SPECIAL 26

Gabriel Khan is a journalist and writer based in Mumbai.

Special 26

Gabriel Khan

HarperCollins *Publishers* India

First published in India by
HarperCollins *Publishers* in 2013

HarperCollins Publishers India, Cyber City, Building 10-A, Gurugram,
Haryana-122002, India
www.harpercollins.co.in

P-ISBN: 978-93-5029-964-7
E-ISBN: 978-93-5029-965-4

2 4 6 8 10 9 7 5 3

Typeset in 11/14 Palatino Linotype
By Saanvi Graphics Noida

Printed and bound at
MicroPrints India, New Delhi

HarperCollins Publishers, Macken House, 39/40 Mayor Street
Upper, Dublin 1, D01 C9W8, Ireland

For my special friend and philosopher,
Shital Bhatia

– Gabriel Khan

Special thanks to Vikram Malhotra and my entire team at Viacom 18 Motion Pictures

– Neeraj Pandey

Contents

Foreword

Literature of the thriller and mystery genre has often been made into cinema. Examples abound from the fictional works of Agatha Christie, Sir Arthur Conan Doyle and, in recent times, Dan Brown. If you turn to the world of real-life crime, Truman Capote's *In Cold Blood* is considered a classic, which was made into a film of the same name by Richard Brooks. Whether it is fact or fiction, the inescapable truth is that successful books have been made into films.

What however sets this book by Gabriel Khan, based on a story by Neeraj Pandey, apart from the rest is that for the first time a real-life incident adapted for a movie is being converted into a novel.

Neeraj Pandey has a knack for gripping audiences with the way he weaves the plot of his films. In his first film, *A Wednesday*, there were several edge-of-the-seat moments. And in *Special 26* too he showcases his craft as a master of the thriller. *Special 26* has its roots in a heist which took place in Bombay, as it was called in 1987, in which a conman perpetrated perhaps the biggest theft of our times, and was never caught. This book captures the essence of that unbelievable true story, in a simple and lucid manner.

When I first heard about the plot, I was staggered by its audacity. And that quality, I understood later when I read up about such tricksters, is essential for any con job to succeed. Whether it was about the man who sold the Eiffel Tower twice – would you believe it? – or the man who sold the Big Ben, it was the audaciousness of the scheme which never made their targets suspect that they were being had.

By any account, these men, and the con artiste in *Special 26*, are men with great mental abilities, though they put that to wrong use.

They are seasoned actors of sorts, have great skills in impersonation and huge reservoirs of confidence. It is remarkable that they carried out such crimes of deception in person in an age when there were no mobile phones, SMS messages or emails. These conveniences of the modern age aid in effectively distancing a criminal from his victim in hoaxes.

These are times when there is a debate on whether films motivate behaviour and inspire crime. These are also times when banks, financial institutions and government agencies are routinely sending out advisories alerting the public against revealing their bank details, or making payments to spurious agencies on receipt of emails and SMS messages promising windfall gains.

Viewed in that context, the readers of this book will benefit twofold: not only will they be entertained, they assuredly will also benefit from the knowledge of how con games are played out in real life.

Anupam Kher
February 2013

Introduction

The robbery at Tribhovandas Bhimji Zaveri on 19 March 1987 still remains one of the biggest and most sensational unsolved cases in the history of the Mumbai Police.

As many as twenty-six so-called probationary CBI officers entered the jewellery shop, announcing that it was being raided. The mastermind strode straight to the shop owner Pratapbhai Zaveri, introduced himself as a CBI officer and produced a search warrant. He ordered that the close-circuit television camera be shut down and that the jeweller surrender his licensed revolver. No telephone calls were allowed as the CBI recruits took cash and samples of ornaments for investigation.

Forty-five minutes later, the conman asked two men to keep the briefcases in a waiting bus. The rest of the 'officers' were asked to guard the shop as the leader left to 'supervise' another raid. He never came back, and was never seen again. The loot roughly amounted to Rs 87 lakh, which in 1987 was an astronomical sum. A background check later revealed that all the hapless recruits had actually answered a classified advertisement two days earlier in a leading daily seeking applicants for the post of 'Security and Intelligence officers'. The Mumbai Police are still clueless about the mysterious conman who knew only too well how the intelligence agency functioned. More shocking is the fact that this robbery is only one, albeit a significantly large one, of the innumerable cases that have gone undetected for decades.

This was never extensively explored or covered except by S. Hussain Zaidi in his crime columns in the *Indian Express* in 1996, where he discussed twenty-six such unsolved crimes.

So when I read the script of *Special 26* by film-maker Neeraj Pandey, I was stunned. It was 4.30 a.m. by the time I finished reading it and I had been reading it for several hours. I sent him a message saying that this was material for a thriller novel.

The story charts the capers of a gang which cons a minister in Delhi, a movie star in Chandigarh, outsmarts a raiding squad of income-tax sleuths in Calcutta and finally reaches Bombay for one last and final heist. The cat-and-mouse game between the fake CBI and the real CBI is one of the most interesting aspects of the story. The gripping story explodes in a riveting climax that will leave the readers stunned. This roller coaster of a movie, *Special 26,* does not allow the viewer to take his eyes off the screen for a second. It took a lot of effort to convince Neeraj that this deserves to be converted into a book. Since the story and screenplay were already in place, not much work or research had to be done.

However, I would like to extend my gratitude and profound thanks to all those who made this book possible. My foremost thanks are reserved for Neeraj Pandey, Shital

Bhatia of Friday Filmworks and Vikram Malhotra of Viacom 18. I would also like to thank Akshay Kumar, Anupam Kher and Manoj Bajpai. I would like to extend my thanks to the entire crew and cast of *Special 26*.

Special thanks for my favourite editor and publisher, V.K. Karthika, and Shantanu Ray Chaudhuri of HarperCollins and Rajni George. I also thank the design team at HarperCollins, which includes Shuka and especially Arijit Ganguly, who tirelessly worked to ensure that we got the exact design with a retro look and did not let up until we got the right one.

Among others who helped with their dedication and sincerity are Aditya Prakash Iengar, Vaibhav Sorte, Bilal Siddique and Subhro Ganguly.

Prologue

19 March 1987.

The four snipers were in place, the tips of their guns converging at the point that marked the entrance of the shop. They were ready.

And so were the men down on the street. The one inside the barbershop. The one at the bus stop. The one near the run-down theatre. Hell, the bootblack was a cop too, and yes, he too was ready.

Waseem Khan stood on the terrace of the four-storey building, his foot resting lightly on the edge as he surveyed his surroundings for the hundredth time. His appraisal might have seemed casual but those who knew him well knew it wasn't casual at all. But then, it wasn't a survey really; it was a scan. An intense, particular reconnaissance with zero room for error.

Deputy Commissioner of the Economic Offences Wing, Waseem Khan was one of the most decorated and revered officers of the Central Bureau of Investigation, New Delhi. He was the go-to guy, the troubleshooter, the man whom the cops, bureaucrats and politicians could count on if they screwed up. God help you if you were a criminal and crossed swords – or paths, for that matter – with Waseem. They said he never lost his man, never gave up on a chase, never blinked.

And this was one chase that they were losing, so they had brought in the best they had.

'They' being the Cop, the Bureaucrat and the Politician.

Waseem looked at the building directly opposite his vantage point. It was as if a giant mirror had mated with some cement, and the result was one of the most shiny, sparkling jewellery storerooms in the city, complete with bright lights, a tasteful neon sign, brilliantly polished glass windows and doors — even the security guard's belt buckle had a bronze mirror. The letters on the board screamed out the name: BHUVANDAS SINGHANIA JEWELLERS. This was one jeweller who had struck gold, thought Waseem, smirking at his own pun.

What the jeweller didn't know was that at that very moment, there were cops inside his brilliant temple to ornamentation. Today, they were jewellery connoisseurs.

Also inside the shop was estimated to be over a couple of crores' worth of gold and jewellery.

This was the bait, and the robbers had already been hooked.

What they didn't know was that it was all fake.

All Waseem had to do now was wait. He took out a Capstan and lit it. It was bliss for four seconds and then the same recurring thought – the government should ban these motherfucking cancer sticks.

He looked around. Bus stop, check. Doshi and Gupte were chatting like two regular office-goers.

Junction at the end of the road, secured.

Bhonsle was standing next to his Yezdi motorcycle, as if waiting for his girlfriend.

Next, the exit to Charni Road station. Rajni and Subhash were chatting at the entrance, posing as two casual smokers.

The main road, check. Lying in wait there was Ranveer Singh, itching for some serious action.

The name popped up in his head once again. Ajay Singh. Singh and his gang were both Unknown and Wanted. And they were not going to escape today.

He'd thought of everything. Men like Waseem hate leaving things to chance. A lot was riding on today's outcome; in fact, his entire career depended on it. He had spent the last five years trying to catch this gang, but they had remained elusive, just out of reach. It had become a matter of prestige for him to nail the sons of bitches, and do it before they fucked him – or someone else – over again.

Yes, he was confident this would be his day. Three days ago, he had found rock-solid proof that the gang would strike here, at Bhuvandas Singhania, one of the biggest jewellers in the city. This would be their fiftieth heist.

Waseem cursed. Fifty times before he had finally been called in!

Not today, suckers, thought Waseem. Today, you're going down. You know why? Because you're up against me.

Down on the street, everything looked exactly as it should. Except that none of it was as it seemed. Even the man in the corner who was getting his shoes polished was part of it; he had too large a bulge in his jacket for someone carrying a book. A holster maybe. Shailesh.

The bootblack polishing Shailesh's shoe kept an eye on everything around him. Ravi. He looked across the street at Nair, and almost smiled. Nair was the coconut man. As he came from Kerala, it was pretty much preordained that he would be the one cutting and serving coconuts. Perhaps he could have practised more, thought Waseem; every scythe of his blade threatened to split open more than just the vulnerable coconut shell.

Waseem looked at his officers one by one. The man on the bench reading the paper. The seemingly unemployed duo chatting on the pavement near the signal. The men at the garage repairing some auto parts. And of course, the men sprinkled inside the building opposite and those inside the shop itself. The place was swarming with police.

Waseem's new watch told him it was just past noon. It even told him what the date was, something he was still getting used to: 19 March.

Just then, a flash of light caught his eye. The man at the traffic lights had given him the signal, flashing the sun off his steel-encased watch right into his chief's eyes. Showtime.

Waseem craned his neck and waited to see what was approaching off the main road. A bus entered his line of sight. There was a subtle change in the atmosphere on the street, as if it was suddenly charged with a kind of purpose.

The bus was full, and it was barely moving. Lumbering slowly along the road, it inched closer and finally came to a halt. It now stood about twenty metres away from the shop.

Waseem smiled, flicked his cigarette to the ground, and stubbed it out with his Bata Ambassador shoes.

This was it. They were all here.

It began now.

1

Law's Raiders

Life was stagnating dangerously when the phone call came and changed Ranveer Singh's life forever.

Ranveer was always looking for something challenging, and the first few days had been depressingly devoid of anything. But something would come along, he was sure of it, an opportunity of some kind or another, and he swore to himself that he would grab it firmly with both hands and wring it so hard that...

He had no idea how to complete that analogy.

Then the phone rang.

'This is Ajay Singh, CBI ward 16, Special Investigations Unit, speaking from Additional Director P.K. Sharma's office.' The voice was smooth and richly layered, one to which Ranveer couldn't say no. If that voice had told him to shoot himself, he would have happily picked up the gun. You couldn't say no to it.

'CBI?' he repeated. Then immediately, he checked himself and said, 'Janab.' The word expressed both respect and surrender.

'We are conducting some very high-profile raids,' Ajay continued. 'For that, we need adequate backup. I need you, three of your men and a woman officer. The best you have, Ranveer. We need three uniformed men and two officers from Safdarjung police station.'

'Only five, sir? Not more?' Ranveer was under the impression that you needed a lot more manpower to carry out a raid.

Ajay clicked his tongue in irritation. 'Yes, five. Five is enough,' he said. 'We don't want to scare them away.'

'Ah, I see sir! We'll be there,' said Ranveer.

Ajay's voice grew distant, and Ranveer could hear a muffled voice speaking from behind wherever Ajay was. Then the man was back on the phone again. 'They have to be your best, Inspector Ranveer. The CBI doesn't work with riff-raff.'

'Of course, sir! I know that, sir!'

'Good. Now, I want you and your people to meet us at the Safdarjung bus stop in fifteen minutes, got it? Don't be late!'

'Sir, yes sir!' Ranveer almost saluted, but checked himself in time. 'Where is the raid, sir?'

'Listen kid, even I don't know where. Only my boss Sharmaji knows. He will tell me when he feels it's time. Meet us at the bus stop. Don't be late.'

Before Ranveer could say anything, the line went dead.

Exactly fifteen minutes after the call, a jeep carrying Ranveer, Shanti – the woman constable – and three others screeched to a halt near the Safdarjung bus stop. A man got out of a spanking white Ambassador parked on the side of the road, and walked towards them. He was a nondescript man: clean-shaven face, drab suit and an utterly forgettable face.

Ranveer and Shanti got out of their Gypsy. The man strode up to them and stuck out his hand. 'Ranveer? I'm Ajay Singh.'

Okay, so this was the Voice. 'Good morning, sir. We're all here, the backup you wanted.'

'Good. Follow us in your vehicle, please,' Ajay said, then turned briskly and headed back to his car.

Fifteen minutes later, the vehicles came to a halt in front of an imposing bungalow. There was a flurry of doors opening and closing, and the two groups converged.

Shanti's face wore a worried expression. 'Anything wrong, constable?' asked Ajay.

'No, sir, nothing!' she said, her face clearing magically.

'Come on, what is it?'

Shanti wrestled with it for a second, and then blurted out, 'Sir, this is Minister Gupta's house!'

Ajay arched an eyebrow. 'And your point is?'

For a moment, Shanti was confused, and then the penny dropped. So did her jaw. 'We're raiding the *minister's* house!'

Ajay smiled enigmatically. 'Ranveer, come with me. I just want to... Sharmaji, this is Ranveer, the officer I told you about.'

The man to whom Ajay had just deferentially introduced Ranveer was a towering behemoth of a man. Everything about him was muscle and intimidation. 'Yes, yes. Ajay, can we get along with this now? I don't want these fuckers to get the chance to hide anything.'

Ranveer stood back, well aware that he was just the hired help. The real deal was the CBI raid that was going to play out in a matter of minutes.

Sharmaji stomped to the gate and flashed his ID card at the security guards. This immediately cleared all potential hurdles, and the gate was flung open. Sharmaji strode over to the portico, saw that the main door was open, and stomped right in, yelling 'CBI' at the top of his lungs, his men Iqbal, Joginder and Ajay in tow; followed by Ranveer, Shanti and three others, who were openly awed by these daring moves.

To the right of the main door was the living room, where Minister Gupta was ensconced in a discussion with his PA. Sharmaji's entry seemed to disturb the PA more than his boss; he scrambled up and hurried over to Sharmaji, flapping his arms in outrage.

'Hey hey hey! What's the meaning of this?'

Ajay rushed forward, holding up a warrant. 'CBI! This is a raid. Please stand back!'

'Fuck off. You can't just barge in here like this! You…'

There was the sound of a resounding slap, and the PA was flung across the room, landing at Minister Gupta's feet, holding a bruised cheek and an even more bruised ego.

'Sir, they're from the CBI all right. I think you're being raided…' His voice trailed off.

The minister hadn't moved. He was still gaping at the men who had barged in. Ajay walked up to him, shoved the warrant into his hand, winked at him, and went to stand next to Sharmaji, who was now barking out orders.

Minister Gupta was mystified. The CBI at his doorstep – impossible! Even the National Security Guards or the Secret Service of the US President wouldn't dare raid his house. How the fuck had these guys sailed in?

Gupta was an entirely self-made man Born into a humble trader's family in Deoria, Uttar Pradesh, he had slaved to make his mark in regional politics. So much so that his manipulative skills in state-level politics soon propelled him on to the national scene.

One of Gupta's mottos was 'bestow and grow'. If you bestowed money on your acolytes and peers, they would help you grow – a principle nobody followed in Indian politics, where sheer power was used to make your subordinates obey you. It was because of his unconventional ideas that, within a span of just twenty-two years, he had risen to become a minister of state in the highly lucrative telecom ministry. And the future was looking bright. They were saying that something called a mobile phone would radically transform this sector – and change the world – in the next few years. No wires, no receivers, nothing. Just a single instrument to carry with you, which you could talk on as you walked! With all that money and power, the future promised, prime ministership beckoned!

But these CBI jokers were hell-bent on ruining his carefully nurtured dreams and aspirations.

'All right, Ajay, start the search. Ranveer, stand guard. Take care of anyone trying to be too smart. I don't care what you do with them, use your imagination. Iqbal, I want the phone lines disconnected right now. You two, watch the road outside, don't let anyone in. Joginder, make sure no one leaves this house either. Move it, move it, move it!'

Within minutes, the house had been worked through. The devastation was at tornado level. But a tornado would have still left some things untouched, owing to the sheer randomness of where it struck. These guys were anything but random. Ranveer watched with admiration as they picked through everything, not missing a single inch.

The first five minutes yielded the usual catch in the usual places — a large amount of cash, gold, jewellery, the lot. But as the search progressed, Ranveer watched open-mouthed as, one by one, the CBI men located hidden nooks and crannies; the next five minutes threw up several gunny bags stuffed with currency.

'What the hell is this, Mantriji? Huh?' Sharmaji bellowed at the harrowed minister. 'Keep searching, boys. There's a lot more here, I can feel it!'

Suddenly, a plaintive wail cut through the noise. It took everyone a minute to place its source, but soon the minister's wife, a lady of epic proportions and an apparently robust set of lungs, came into view.

'Why are you all here? What do you all want from us? My husband is a good man! Why are you doing this to him?' she howled, as she slowly made her way through the room.

Ajay was following her with a ferociously determined expression. 'The key, madam. I need the key to this almirah, please.' He gestured to a large almirah at the centre of the room.

The woman paused in her yowling, looked at Ajay, sniffed and said, 'It's lost.'

'Are you sure, ma'am?'

'Of course! Why do you want the key? Darling, why do they want the key?' She took up her howling again, directing it at her husband now. At this point, the minister was sitting on a couch, his head in his hands. Ranveer almost felt sorry for him. Almost.

Sharmaji had been a spectator as the drama unfolded; he took charge again. Walking towards the almirah whose key was apparently lost, he paused for a moment – and then, without warning, he kicked the door in. It smashed to pieces. Everyone watched as more cash, gold and jewellery came tumbling out: glittering confirmation of the minister's guilt.

There was a pregnant pause as the mistress of the house surveyed the almirah's guilt-laden contents, her eyes wide. Then, heaving with fury that seemed to well up from deep within, she turned on her husband. 'You! Where did you get all this? When did you bring this here? And how could you not tell me! I can't believe you didn't tell me!'

'All right, all right,' Sharmaji's voice immediately quietened the room. 'Iqbal, make an inventory of everything we've found.'

He then turned to the minister. 'Mr Gupta, it seems we've caught you with your pants down.'

For a second, Gupta considered pulling a few strings, calling his friends in the CBI or the Ministry of Home Affairs. But he refrained. It would only help spread the word, and then the shit would really hit the roof. Much better to end this here and now.

Gupta took a deep breath, and said, 'Umm, sir, can I speak with you in private, please?'

A frigid silence followed, broken only by the sound of Iqbal's pen scratching on paper. Gupta folded his hands. 'Please, sir.'

Sharmaji nodded almost imperceptibly. Relief flooding his face, Gupta led him out of the room to the hallway, followed closely by the PA, who kept his distance from Sharmaji.

'Sir, my PA is a moron. He has no idea how to talk to people, especially to an important officer like you! Please forgive him.'

Sharmaji stood still, hands folded across his chest.

Beads of sweat appeared on Gupta's face. 'Sir, please try and understand. You're an important man, you know how it all works. This will kill my career, I don't know what I'll do. Please try and—'

Sharmaji interrupted. 'How much?'

'Eh?' Gupta said, surprised, not daring to hope that there might be a way out for him so early in the process.

'How much are you offering me, Mantriji?'

A sly smirk stretched Gupta's face. 'Well, officer, for someone like you, I think we can settle at two lakh—'

He never finished the sentence. Sharmaji's arm was a blur as it cut through the air and, to everyone's horror, landed palm first on the fat left cheek of the minister. It was still reverberating when another one landed on the right cheek. Unable to speak, shocked more at the ignominy of having been slapped – he, a minister! – than the pain from the blow itself, Gupta fell prostrate at Sharmaji's feet.

'P.K. Sharma. Remember that name, you miserable fuck. And tell your friends they'd better pray the CBI doesn't raid their houses, and if it does, that P.K. Sharma doesn't come to visit. I know you're crooked, bhenchod, and I'm going to put you behind bars,' Sharmaji said through gritted teeth, menace in every syllable. 'Iqbal?'

'Sir!'

'Is the list ready?'

'Yes, sir.'

'Get this bastard to sign it. The rest of you, get all this stuff outside, pronto.' He strode out.

The PA appeared quietly behind the minister. 'Good thing you offered him just two, sir.'

Two and a half hours later, the raid was finally over. All the seized cash, jewellery, gold and various assets were piled high in the centre of the courtyard.

'All right, get all this stuff to the police station. Load it up in the car.' Sharmaji beckoned to Ranveer, who was watching, mouth agape.

'Ranveer, get onto the wireless and inform your chowki that Joginder and Iqbal are on their way with the goods.'

'Yes, sir.' Ranveer passed on the rapid-fire command to Nihal Singh, one of the constables. Nihal went off and Ranveer watched Joginder place a wad of papers under Sharmaji's nose – which he signed obediently.

'All right, Joginder. Get all this stuff to the chowki, lodge an FIR, get the inventory done and get your ass back here. You have thirty minutes. Come back and get Ranveer's signature on the GMD,' Sharmaji said.

'Yes, sir,' said Joginder. He drove off in the car which bore the confiscated goods, along with Iqbal.

Sharmaji continued, 'Ranveer, you'll stay here on guard for now. Joginder will file the FIR and come back with the GMD. You will sign — what's the matter?'

Sharmaji finally noticed that Ranveer was looking a little queasy, and took pity on him. 'Was this your first raid?' he said kindly.

Ranveer nodded, unable to speak.

Sharmaji chuckled. 'So, how did you like it?'

Ranveer glanced over at the portico, where the stunned and broken Gupta was still standing with his family. 'Sir, it was brilliant! I've become your fan, sir! The way you broke that corrupt man… Today I found out the power of honesty. Thank you, sir,' gushed Ranveer, knowing he was voicing the sentiments of the four Safdarjung cops behind him.

Sharmaji grew serious. 'Listen, Ranveer, never forget one thing. True strength lies in your heart. Never ever doubt your heart.'

Ranveer choked up, unable to respond, and simply nodded.

'Sir, we're done,' said Ajay, walking up behind Sharmaji.

'All right, Ranveer. We'll be off, there are more raids to take care of. Wait here for Joginder, sign the GMD, and you'll be done too, okay?' Sharmaji said, putting a hand on Ranveer's shoulder.

Ranveer smiled proudly. 'Yes, sir. Thank you, sir.'

2

Chase

'Get out of the way! Get the *fuck* out of the way!'

I yelled at the top of my voice at the people milling about. I was trying to catch up with the man running a few hundred yards ahead of me. We were running on a Monday morning in Connaught Place and there were many reasons I wanted to catch up with him. The most important one – he was running *away* from me. That, and he had a gun in his hand.

My mind was racing as I ran, dodging the people my target kept pushing out of his way; it was automatically taking in details of the surroundings, telling me I couldn't risk a shootout here. Too many people, too dangerous. I just hoped I would catch the man I knew only as Gupta before he figured out his advantage and got himself a hostage, a nice ticket out of this mess.

I chased Gupta down an alley, and then into the next street. All I had on was a white vest and pyjamas, and I knew that nobody would be able to tell that I was a cop chasing a bad guy. All they saw was a man with a gun being chased by a man without a gun. Mine was still tucked securely into the belt I wore under my pyjamas.

My wife would not have been amused.

I was in shape and lethal on foot, so I felt a grim sense of satisfaction in knowing that Gupta would not be able to lose me. He knew it too, but he tried to slow me down through the usual little tricks: shoving the men he was running past so that they fell into my path. I had to dodge, jump and leapfrog my way over the human obstacle course, but grew used to it; all the while, I was gaining ground.

Other cops had joined the chase too, but were lagging behind, weighed down by their potbellies and general unfamiliarity with physical exertion. I was far ahead of them – but at least I wasn't alone. My faithful subordinate Rahul was just behind me, and also running hard. And there was a new guy huffing along behind Rahul. I didn't know the fellow, but he seemed intelligent and enthusiastic thus far.

Well, we'll see, I thought, as I closed in on my quarry.

Gupta suddenly turned in mid-stride and I stopped in my tracks – looking down the barrel of a gun trembling in his hand not twenty feet away.

'Get down, everybody *get down*!' I yelled.

Like all crowds, this one was slow to react. I saw the man take aim, and knew he was going to miss me. But the way he was aiming, he wouldn't miss the petrified schoolboy quivering next to me.

Still yelling, I threw myself at the kid and pinned him to the ground – just as a shot rang out. I heard the bullet whistling over my head, and covered the child with my body to protect him from the continued gunfire. The bullets struck something; I heard the sound of glass shattering.

Finally, the crowd perceived they were in grave danger and began to scream and run away. Fucking idiots. Here was a guy shooting straight into the crowd and instead of falling flat on the ground to avoid his wild bullets, all they could do was run around bawling their heads off.

I looked up finally when the shooting ceased, and saw Gupta set off, on the run again. I picked myself up, off the boy, checked that he was unhurt, and began to run again. Just then, I heard a plaintive voice. 'You broke my car!'

The kid was holding a broken toy car in his hand which seemed to hold his attention. No matter that he had just been saved from debilitating injury, gruesome death, trauma, or all of the above.

Gratitude. Bloody hell. Now *this* my wife would definitely find amusing.

I started off in pursuit of bloody Gupta again.

Finally, the man figured out he was in way too deep. There was no car coming to his rescue, he couldn't find a dark alley or corner to hide in because it was daytime, and he had at least thirty cops on his tail. Including me. He wasn't going anywhere.

Stopping abruptly in the middle of the square like a little video game figure, he grabbed a girl.

Damn! He'd done exactly what I had anticipated. He'd got himself a hostage.

The immediate vicinity of the square emptied swiftly this time. In a matter of seconds, only Gupta and the girl were left standing in its centre, his left arm around her throat; the gun in his right hand pointed at her head.

'Stop! Stop right there!' he yelled. 'You move and I shoot her.'

I stood still, my right hand rigid behind me as it fixed on the butt of my own gun, which nestled between the belt and my body. The crowd had started running, true, but with the morbid fascination that is the trait of all humanity, they hadn't gone far. Now, they stood some fifty feet away, forming a semi-circle around us, the idiots. As though they were watching a movie.

Out of the corner of my eye, I saw that the other cops had all arrived, most of them panting and severely out of breath. They were all around the crowd, restraining people. The fittest of the lot, who had managed to keep up with the chase, were at the head of the circle, just behind me, guns raised and pointing straight at Gupta's head.

The wind blew through this spectacle gently, and nothing else moved. It was as silent as death.

'I'm serious! I'll kill her if you move!' Gupta shouted again manically, spit flowing from his paan-encased lips.

'Really, Gupta? You're going to shoot her? And then what? She's dead and you don't have a shield. We've got you, man,' I said, deliberately taunting him. I had to buy enough time for Gupta to make a mistake. It didn't have to be much, just the slightest slip was all I needed.

'Shut up, shut up!' Gupta screamed hysterically. 'You think I won't kill her? I will... none of you move!'

I spoke softly. 'Everyone, we need this maniac alive. He's too valuable to lose.'

I could feel the men around me stiffen with surprise. On my right, Rahul whispered, 'Sir! But the girl?'

'I know, you idiot. Just don't make any sudden movements. I'll handle this,' I whispered, not looking away from Gupta's crazed eyes.

'Okay, Gupta. What do you want?' I said in a louder voice. I had to keep him talking, get him to make that mistake I was looking for. They always made a mistake, if you knew what you were doing.

He'd obviously not thought this through. 'Just stay where you are!' he screamed again.

'I'm not moving. None of us is moving. Take it easy. You don't have a way out of here,' I said in an even tone. The girl was whimpering now, large tears rolling from her eyes and smudging kohl across her cheeks. The gun was still jabbed against her temple.

'Sure I do! You're not going to do anything as long as I'm holding this bitch!'

Trouble. This guy was fast losing it.

'Why don't you just give up?' I asked conversationally. 'I promise we won't treat you badly. Because you see, if you kill that girl, we *will* kill you. No doubt. But if you let her go, and come quietly with me, I promise I won't hurt you.'

'No, no, no! All right, all of you put your guns down!' Gupta yelled, looking from me to the officers around me. 'Right now!'

My eyes were on the gun. It hadn't left the girl's head.

'Okay, slowly now, lower your weapons,' I said, eyes pinned to Gupta and the gun.

'Sir?' Rahul asked from my left, clearly confused by my order.

'I said, lower your weapons,' I hissed between clenched teeth. Come on, I thought furiously, give me anything. Just one opening, that's all.

The men around me slowly lowered their guns. To their credit, they didn't drop them.

Gupta's eyes swung back to me, and his lips twisted into a crazy smile. He brought the gun around quickly and pointed it at me, away from the girl. She was safe, and in the space of two minutes, I was staring down the barrel of the same gun.

Time seemed to slow down; even as my already heightened senses screamed every detail at me with increasingly vivid clarity. I saw Gupta's finger start to squeeze the trigger; the barrel flinched as the casing turned into place, and the hammer rose.

My reflexes took over. In one swift motion, I fell to my knees and brought my hand around with my service revolver in it.

The hammer slammed into place. My knees hit the ground and the gun roared, the bullet screaming its way towards me. I brought my hand up.

The bullet went through the exact spot where I'd been standing a fraction of a second earlier.

I didn't pause as my hand swept a wide arc from behind my back. Halfway through the arc, I squeezed the trigger.

My mind had already taken aim. And its aim was true.

The bullet smashed into Gupta's knee. He screamed and fell back, trying to clutch at the girl. But she had already broken free of him as he began his unsteady descent, and ran towards the crowd, sobbing uncontrollably.

Gupta fell to the ground, howling in pain. He had lost his hold on the gun, and it had clattered away and come to rest a few feet from him.

The men around me moved swiftly to accost Gupta. One of them picked up the gun and came to me. It was Rahul. He spoke almost reverentially, 'Sir, are you all right?'

'Of course! I'm fine,' I said. I got back to my feet and started barking out orders. 'Take Gupta into custody, and someone try and calm down that girl. I want ten men to clean up this area now and control the crowd. Rahul, get on the wireless and call for an ambulance. Gupta's not going anywhere now.'

'Yes, sir,' said Rahul and dashed off.

My role here was over. As I was walking away, I heard the new kid whisper to someone else, 'Man, this guy is the real deal! Did you see what he just did?'

I could tell that he was awed by what he had just witnessed, and judging by the faces of the others around, they were pretty impressed too.

I smiled to myself. A job well done.

3

Games of Fate

His heart thudded, pounding its protest and registering his fear against the wall of his chest. He could see all the way down, right down to the street, three storeys below. Well, not the whole street, only the parts of it that were bathed in the bright circle of light falling from the streetlamp. The rest was all swallowed up by night. If he fell, he might melt into that blackness. Or maybe not.

This was not a place to be, thought Ajay. This was not the place for a fourteen-year-old. What the hell was he thinking?

When he'd planned this earlier, it had seemed so easy, so clear! Of course, that was down there, with the safety of the ground beneath his feet and the daylight lending him a fickle bravado. Right now, it was flickering unsteadily under the steady contemplation of night.

For some months now, this downtown neighbourhood had been suffering from an uptown affliction – burglary. For some strange reason, the thieves seemed to have tired of breaking into mansions and palaces and stealing valuable stuff, and were trying their hand at robbing the less rich, less fortunate families of the slums of Sion Koliwada. Maybe they were just practising their skills on easier targets, because of course people here didn't have fancy alarms and jigsaw locks. They did, however, have a propensity to run down an escaping burglar with sticks and hammers and shovels and cricket bats and whatever else would assist the breaking of a few bones. But then, that was an occupational hazard.

A wide-eyed Ajay had heard the stories, listened to the grown-ups in the neighbourhood speak of how the law didn't care for them, didn't bother if some poor family got robbed. Nothing in it for them, they would say, why should they care? But Ajay knew that wasn't the truth. A long time ago, before his mother had walked out on them and his father had gone all silent and broody, he had told Ajay that all the cops in this part of town were lower down the ladder, with cheap and greasy palms. Anyone else would have generalized from there on, applied this to their own unfortunate situation and then to the rest of the police system, but not Ajay. He believed, albeit vaguely, that when it came to the big stuff like fighting for the country, or perhaps even the big money, the cops in the better part of town, at least, wouldn't be the same. They would be honest, upright and principled. It wasn't a feeling that went around a lot in this area, but it kept him going. And he would prove it. He would catch the robber himself, hand him over to the police and show them that the law could be trusted.

So, he'd spent that whole week planning and practising. He'd even skipped his homework after coming home from school, and it still nagged at him, that there was a pile of arithmetic problems he hadn't yet solved. But what he was doing was for the greater common good, wasn't it? He was helping to protect the neighbourhood. And that meant he was helping his country. He was one of the good guys!

None of that worked up here, in this enveloping nothingness of night; there was barely enough moon in the dark sky to help him make out shapes. Shadows and shapes were scary, sure, but this near jet-black darkness was scarier. It was dawning on the teenager that his plan might not be the best.

But he was here now, and he would wait it out. He slowed down his breathing, trying to calm his mind, the way he'd learned to do when he missed his mother, or every time he found his father sitting still, wrapped up in his sorrow, staring into nothing. His beating heart steadied, his hands stopped trembling, and the sound of the blood pounding in his ears gave way to the noise of the night.

Ajay usually loved night-time. True, he had never spent it all alone on top of a building in a potentially dangerous situation, but from the safety of his room, he would listen for hours to the night speaking to him – the bark of a dog, the snores of the old man next door, the distant sound of car engines, the passing of a train, the occasional chirping of a hesitant cricket, the hoot of an owl.

Slowly, as Ajay came back from somewhere beyond the fear to himself, the sounds returned to him and the familiar night welcomed him. Though it was still a bit darker than he liked it, the sounds were all here. Well, maybe not of the owl.

Just as he was beginning to enjoy himself, a shadow moved nearby, and things suddenly got very real.

On the roof opposite him, a man was moving silently. Ajay couldn't make out his features, but a man wearing black, carrying a black bag and moving stealthily over a rooftop in the dead of night signified only one thing. This guy was up to no good.

To his surprise, Ajay realized he wasn't petrified – which he would have been a few minutes earlier at the thought of black-clad men, carrying black bags and moving stealthily on rooftops. His heart *was* beating faster, but this time there was no fear. Only the anticipation of executing a well-laid plan.

He stuck out a foot, and very carefully dislodged a tile, not enough to make a loud noise that would alert anybody else, but enough to catch the man's attention. The tile grated against another, and there was a sharp intake of breath. The man was now looking directly at him. His hand moved, and there was a flash of steel. A knife appeared in his hand.

All right, thought Ajay. Come on. You and me, over these roofs. Come on, catch me if you can.

Moving slowly, the man slung the bag over his shoulder. Then, with a low growl, knife outstretched, he leaped across the narrow gap.

The knife swished through the air, but Ajay was already scrambling up and running over the roof, his bare feet making hardly any noise. The man followed him.

Ajay ran to the edge and vaulted over the low wall, landing on his feet, and was up and running again in a second. Behind him, the man jumped over the wall, clearing it without difficulty.

Ajay ran on, dodging through the washing hanging on the clotheslines, ducking and weaving through the wires that dangled at varying heights. He had spent all his life on these roofs, often being scolded off them.

He never really liked playing with the other boys, and they thought him strange because he liked his books better than a football. But his solitary wanderings had familiarized him with the exact placement of the roofs, their layout, and how the clothes were hung out to dry, who hung what out and where.

His follower didn't know any of this. Soon, Ajay heard him fumbling with the clothes, flinging them out of his way as he tried to catch up. There went Mrs Chavan's new sari across the parapet, followed by Mr Aiyar's veshti, trampled underfoot. The Aptes' clothesline was well-placed, allowing the shorter boy to duck beneath neatly and then almost taking his pursuer's head off when he barrelled along immediately afterwards and ran straight into it. But the man was relentless, getting back on his feet immediately.

Ajay didn't hesitate once. He made his way out of the laundry-laden maze of hazards, ran to the edge of the roof, and without breaking stride, leaped, sailed through the air and landed on the parapet of the next roof. He knew the man would follow him – it wasn't a big gap – and sure enough, five seconds later, he heard the grunt as the man landed.

Ajay ran on. Right here, left here, duck under the pipe, right again, duck under the tank, get up, jump the gap, down the ladder, left, keep going, almost there, almost there. The man kept coming, and he was gaining ground.

Right, left, straight dash, then right by the water tank, and stop *now*!

There it was, the yawning eight-foot gap leading straight down into the unused warehouse. The place was full of planks of wood and buckets, and every noisy thing Ajay could find. He flung himself down behind a barrel and waited.

The man saw Ajay making the blind turn ten feet in front of him and ran harder. He came out of the turn at full speed and saw two things.

One: Ajay grinning at him from behind a barrel to his right.

Two: the gap right in front, which he'd had no way of seeing until it was too late.

He fell, crashing into the planks and the empty steel buckets, creating a noise that was heard across at least three buildings. Down, down, down, falling, breaking a few planks and denting a couple of mugs along the way, the man landed on the ground amidst raining wood and steel, dazed and hurt but quite alive.

Within minutes, people were up and about, not a single hand without a makeshift weapon improvised from household paraphernalia. From above, Ajay watched them pick the man up bodily, understanding at once what he was up to, and dealing him a few blows. But then, seeing he was pretty banged up anyway, they dragged him away towards the local police station, a few people doling out a few half-hearted blows en route just for the heck of it. Nobody noticed the satisfied boy watching from the top of the warehouse.

That satisfaction stayed with Ajay right until the day he started his first job. After that, it turned into something else.

With his father's help – meaning that he hadn't said an outright no – Ajay put himself through college, paying his fees with the help of odd jobs and errands while the other boys were out in the fields playing cricket. His eidetic memory and prodigious intelligence earned him recognition among the teachers but did not impress his peers; typically, he was known only as the super-intelligent geek who kept to himself, a born loner.

Some tried to befriend him, but were always gently dislodged and shunned, though never rudely.

To tell the truth, Ajay wasn't interested in making friends, not just then. He had discovered his passion, and was trying to see if it would find him a job with the country's lawmen. And anyway, those who approached him were clearly doing so out of curiosity more than a spirit of genuine friendship. After a couple of times, Ajay gave up trying to find someone who could actually *interest* him. Sure, the girls were pretty and the guys had lots of money, but none of them understood him, and it didn't take long for them to be exposed in their mediocrity.

Finally, with a sparkling academic profile and an unblemished record under his belt, Ajay approached the CBI.

He had long sought to join the elite investigating agency. Common sense told him that he would be better off trying for the local police force, but his passion led him to sit for the entrance and aptitude exams for CBI recruitment. On the day of the exam, his trepidation as he waited with thousands for the question paper, finally turned into delight as he wrote the exam, knowing he would crack it with ease. A few days later, he got the score – he was among the top twenty.

But Fate can be cruel to the innocent. For despite his intelligence, Ajay was still naive.

Not for long.

One fine October morning, Ajay strode confidently into the interview room, where the candidates who had qualified in the written test were being tested. There were two men in the room, sitting at a table. Ajay sat down in the chair opposite them.

One of them spoke. 'So, Mr Singh, you scored brilliantly in your exam.'

Ajay smiled. 'Thank you, sir.'

'You seem confident. Do you think you can crack this interview?'

'I hope so, sir.'

'Good. Why do you want to join the CBI?'

'To serve my country, sir! To uphold the law and fight for justice!' Ajay's answer was instant, no hesitations.

'Good, good. And how do you propose to do that?'

Ajay's answer was not so quick this time, but he was still not unsure. 'I shall be truthful, honest and just. I shall follow the law and live by its rules. And after my training, I shall stick by what I have learned and try to do what I've been taught, sir.'

The other man spoke. 'Mr Singh, do you have fifty thousand rupees?'

This was unexpected. Ajay's face screwed up in puzzlement. 'Fifty thousand rupees, sir? What for?'

'That is for us to know. Do you have fifty thousand rupees?'

This was difficult territory for Ajay. He earned barely a hundred rupees a month doing odd jobs, and he spent it to keep his father and himself fed and clothed. He said, 'I'm sorry, sir, I don't have the money on me now.'

'That's too bad, kid. Thank you for coming,' the man said, and looked down at the papers in front of him dismissively.

Ajay was thunderstruck. He couldn't understand what was going on. Why the money? He knew they'd checked him out, they knew his background, they knew he didn't have the money. But wait! 'Is this a test, sir?' he said, smiling uncertainly.

The first man spoke again. 'No, this isn't a

test. Either you have the money or you don't. If you don't, you can leave.'

'But why, sir? I scored well in the exam. I promise you, sir, I will make you proud, just give me a chance!' Somewhere deep down, Ajay realized with a shock that he was pleading with them, something he had never done in his life.

'We don't care what you make us feel. Please leave. There's no need for you to come back.'

Something shifted into place in Ajay's brain; he was beginning to understand now. He said, 'What if I have the money, sir? What if I can get it for you?'

'Then we might have a deal.'

He finally realized what was happening. 'So if I can get you the money, you will select me?' he asked, his hands slowly clenching.

'We might be... persuaded, yes. Our approval doesn't come cheap, Mr Singh.'

Ajay stood up. 'Are you asking me for a bribe?' he said through gritted teeth.

'Careful what you say, you little piece of shit. You don't want to get us angry,' the second man said, malice dripping from his voice.

Ajay couldn't believe what he was hearing. This was the CBI! They were supposed to be the best. They upheld the law, and made sure that justice was served, every time. This was all upside down.

He looked at the two men in front of him very carefully. He wouldn't forget them. 'We will meet again,' he said softly, and turned and walked out of the room.

Outside, he felt he could breathe again. But for the first time since his mother had left them for some hotshot jeweller, Ajay felt the pain of betrayal. It was a great effort, but he steeled himself and said out loud, 'They're crooked!'

The very men who were supposed to uphold the law, to be inviolate and upright, were corrupt!

The interview shook Ajay to his core. For nearly a week he remained lost in thought, and in that time, the innocence won through. He decided to try elsewhere.

But Fate wasn't done yet. Over the next month, everywhere he went, every avenue he tried, he came up with the same result.

The police force found him lacking in stature. They told him he was an inch shorter than the regulations prescribed.

The railway police told him his academic record was too good, that he would be wasted on them. Finally, observing his persistence, the interviewer asked him if he would take a bribe.

'Of course not!' Ajay said indignantly.

'That's why we can't hire you.'

Even the customs department turned him down, saying he was 'unrecruitable'.

None of it made sense. Were they all crooked? This was the one thought that assaulted his mind constantly. 'Do I *have* to be like that?' a broken Ajay finally asked Gautam Singhania, the interviewer on the customs board.

The man looked genuinely sorry. 'I'm sorry, Ajay, there's nothing I can do. My hands are tied.'

Through the haze, the smog of emotions, the sentence penetrated to Ajay's consciousness. 'What do you mean, your hands are tied?' he said.

Now Singhania looked uncomfortable. 'Look here, you can't ask such questions. We're done. Thank you for coming,' he said, getting up and walking to the door.

Ajay leaped up, slammed the door shut,

grabbed Singhania by the lapel and shoved him against the wall. 'You tell me what you meant, or I promise I'll hurt you more than you can imagine,' he said, his teeth clenched, his voice low, his hand pressed hard against the man's throat.

Singhania saw the crazed look in Ajay's eyes, debated between candidness and reticence for a second before settling for the former. 'We were instructed not to hire you!' he squeaked.

Ajay was stunned, but he didn't let go. He wanted answers, and by God he was going to get them! 'Who?'

'Come on, I can't tell you that! It'll cost me my job!'

Ajay squeezed harder until Singhania's face turned purple. 'A.K. Gupta! Telecom minister A.K. Gupta!'

Ajay let go, and the man sank to the floor, massaging his bruised throat. But Ajay wasn't done yet. He knelt down in front of Singhania, and said, 'Why?'

'Because he doesn't like you,' the interviewer said reluctantly. 'You misbehaved with his men at the CBI. He wants to get even.'

'WHY?' Ajay roared.

'His brother-in-law. He wanted his brother-in-law to be selected! He paid a huge amount to make sure. Everyone knows that, it's an open secret.'

'So? Why did they screw me?'

'You were one of the best,' Singhania said in a low voice. 'He would never have been selected if he'd come up against you. So you had to be eliminated from the competition.'

Ajay was aghast. That was it? That was why his life, his dream, was being snatched away from him? 'But that was the CBI! Why is nobody else hiring me?'

Singhania sighed. 'You accused them of being crooked?'

'Of course I did! Those bastards—'

'That's why. Ajay, don't you see? You showed your hand too early. You insulted them, and that means that indirectly you insulted the minister too. So they marked you, and that's why nobody will hire you.'

Singhania could see the bewilderment on Ajay's face, but there was something else there too, something he couldn't quite put his finger on.

Ajay clenched his fists. So a minister had wanted his relative to get the job and bribed his way into it, leaving honest, upright men like him out on the streets. Maybe he wasn't the only one, maybe there were others who were suffering like him, just because of that one man. And he was a minister! He was supposed to be helping people, working for them. And the CBI – they were supposed to be for the people, not against them!

Deep inside Ajay, something snapped. The stricken Singhania saw it happen in the youth's eyes.

Leaving the interviewer on the floor, Ajay strode out of the room.

4

The Hound Joins the Hunt

I thanked God again that she had married me. Her father had asked my father and that's how it had happened, but all that didn't matter any more. She was now my wife, the mother of our child. In a rare intimate moment after a week of running around at all hours, here I was finally, in bed with her close to me. Her body was perfect, her touch so soft and sensuous, her eyes brimming with invitation.

'Why are you looking at me like that?'

'Like what?'

'Like you're hungry?'

'You like hungry?'

'I like hungry.'

I reached out and had just caught her by the waist when the hellish ring of the telephone interrupted. Damn! Who would call so early in the morning?

I picked up the phone, barked a furious hello into it, and immediately wished I hadn't. The voice on the other side was the additional director of the CBI, my boss. 'Why are you yelling? Bad time, is it?'

'Not at all, sir. Can you hold for a moment?'

I covered the mouthpiece with my hand and shouted furiously under my breath, 'Fuck fuck fuck, really, really bad time, asshole!'

The hungry thoughts had evaporated. Sana got up and checked herself in the mirror. The dupatta went back to its original position. I went back to mine.

'Sorry, sir. I was getting ready.'

'Good. I want you in my office first thing. Be here by nine,' he said, and hung up.

Bloody hell. That left me barely enough time to take Akbar to the bus stop for his school pickup, get ready and leave. 'Jaan—' I gulped.

'It's all right. I know,' she said, and stalked off.

Half an hour later, Akbar was ready for school and we were on our way to the bus stop, Akbar bouncing on my shoulder.

'Papa! Have you seen Junaid's car?'

'You shouldn't be comparing, Akbar.'

'It's so big! Papa, I want that car! Buy me that car, Papa!'

It hurt a little, that I couldn't even buy a toy for my son. That rich bastard in the house opposite kept buying his son Junaid all the latest toys and gadgets, the whole damn neighbourhood ogling at the spectacle. He'd even got him his own little radio. Parents these days... They don't know what they're doing, and end up spoiling their children.

Akbar kept up his plaintive wailing. 'Papa! I want that car! Will you buy me Gems? I want that car and Gems?'

I bounced him a little more to distract him as I hurried to the bus stop. If we missed the bus, I'd have to take him all the way to school on the scooter, and there was no time for that. The CBI's AD himself had called me in for a chat. Every chat was a potential case and every case was a potential promotion, which in my case was long overdue.

There! Made it in time. The bus hadn't left yet.

'There you go! Be a good boy, have your tiffin. Don't get into a fight like last week—'

'I want that car, PAPA!'

'Behave yourself, Akbar. You be a good boy, and we'll see about that car, all right?' I hated having to bribe the kid, but there was nothing else I could think of to keep him quiet.

I watched Akbar getting into the bus with his friends. At the window, he yelled, 'Bye Dad!'

'Hey! Call me Papa, not Dad!' Who calls their father 'dad'? All this new-age nonsense that kids pick up these days, really! God knows where they get it from.

A hurried breakfast and a mad dash on my scooter later, I was outside the AD's cabin – within the hour, sweating profusely in the June heat. I had been here many times, mostly to be given all kinds of cases that seemed unsolvable. And to be honest, I'd been lucky, and solved pretty much all of them. Sure, I'd had luck on my side. But somehow they'd all worked out. Somehow, I'd found that one thing that helped put all the pieces of the case together. Waseem Khan, CBI Deputy Commissioner, Economic Offences

Wing. And all I had to show for it was a great reputation in the force, a family I hardly ever met, and a salary with which I couldn't even buy a toy for my son. Life's screwed like that. But there's always tomorrow.

As I waited, I ran through all the cases that I'd heard of recently. A couple of homicides, a few hit-and-runs, a high-profile drug bust where a politician was involved. I knew one of them would come my way.

It turned out to be none of the above.

An underling opened the door and ushered me into the AD's office. It was less hot inside; the room even had one of those new air coolers that all the top officers were getting themselves.

The AD looked up. 'Ah, Waseem Khan! Just the man I wanted to see. Have a seat, have a seat.'

Yep, it was a case all right. All the courtesy and sweet talk meant he was going to throw another one at me. One that would have baffled many.

'Thank you, sir,' I said, and sat down across the table.

The AD got straight to the point. 'Have you heard of the 26 January case?'

Of course! How could I have forgotten that one! It was pathetic, actually.

'Yes, sir. Some men raided A.K Gupta's house in our name. Fucked the minister up royally.'

'Exactly. Haven't you wondered why he hasn't lodged a case yet?'

'No, sir.'

'Strange. You don't want to know?'

'Oh, I *know* why he hasn't, sir. It's pretty obvious, isn't it? If he lodges a case, he has to reveal what's been stolen, but then that's stuff you don't want people to know you have at home, because if you do, your career's over.' I was a little impatient. This was a small-time job. Why had he called me in for this?

'Well, you're really cued in, aren't you, Khan?'

'Yes, sir.' It was true. Why be modest where you don't need to be?

'Well, you know there won't be a police case, right?'

'Yes, sir. Sir, why are we bothering with this? It's just a two-bit job, not for the CBI, right?'

'I wish. You know they took the police for a proper ride too?'

'Yes, sir,' I said, as contemptuously as I could. 'With respect, if a cop can be so easily fooled, he doesn't deserve to be a cop.'

'Maybe, maybe.'

'I don't see why the CBI needs to bother with this trivial matter, sir.'

The AD sighed. 'I want to show you something, Khan. Come here.' He got up and went to the window to his right. I went with him.

'See that man there? He's the one those bastards took for a ride.'

I peered through the glass, interested. The man I saw was sitting hunched on a chair, the picture of dejection. Twirling his cap nervously in his hands, he was talking to my man Rahul.

The AD went back to his chair and sat down. 'He's a promising kid,' he said.

I turned back to him. 'How can you say that, sir? He must be a dimwit to have been duped like that!'

'Give him a chance, Khan. He's good. In fact, he has taken the whole thing very seriously, apparently staking his reputation on it.'

I came back and sat down. 'What's left of it, you mean.'

The AD smiled. 'You're a brilliant officer, Khan, and I've wanted to say this to you for a very long time. You're wrong.'

He passed a file to me. 'Read that. That kid went on the hunt, started sniffing around by himself. He dug up all that dirt on his own.'

I glanced through the report, and I had to admit, it was impressive. And as I read it, I realized why the AD had called me in.

'See? In the last year, these guys have pulled off thirteen heists. *Thirteen*! And that's just the ones we know about. Fuck knows how many more places they robbed that we have no clue about.'

'What about the victims, sir?'

'That's the strange part! Half the time, they don't file complaints. Probably crooked themselves, I don't know. But look at the list, Khan. They've impersonated every goddamn agency! CBI, income tax, ACB, everyone. And they're getting away with it.'

I looked up, already knowing the answer to the question I was going to ask. 'What do you want me to do, sir?'

'You know what I want. We have to catch this gang. They're making us look really bad.

People are talking, and they're not saying anything good. This has to stop. *You* have to stop it.'

I looked at the report again. Madras, Nagpur, Trivandrum, Lucknow— these guys were everywhere. And they were targeting mostly businessmen and politicians, every one of them crooked. Obviously, they weren't going to file cases, but word got around.

'Many politicians in here, sir?'

The AD nodded.

'Which party?'

'Take your pick. They're all there.'

Yeah, this case was big. There was only one answer I could give, and he knew it. 'Okay, sir. I'll take over.'

The AD exhaled. 'Good, good. Khan, this nuisance has to end *now*. I'm counting on you.'

'Yes, sir.'

I got up and walked to the door. But before leaving, there was one last thing I had to ask. 'Sir, is there any word on my promotion yet? And the increment?'

Got you, I thought. You can't say no now, not when you want my help.

As expected, the AD immediately nodded. 'Yes, yes, of course. Don't worry, Khan, I'm already on it.'

'Thank you, sir. The kid needs toys that I can't afford with my current pay, sir. I really wouldn't want to have to stoop to asking for bribes.'

With that parting shot, I walked out, not giving him a chance to think of a comeback.

I walked over to the cubicle where Ranveer was sitting with Rahul. With them now was a beggar, reclining in a chair as if he owned the place, and smoking a cigarette.

All three of them sprang to their feet as I approached. I sat down, saying nothing at first. Rahul, having worked with me for several years now, sensed my mood, and kept quiet too. The beggar sat with us, looking from face to face.

'Shankar, will you leave us please?'

The beggar jumped up. 'Sorry, sir,' he said, and went to his desk, took out a holster hidden beneath the rags, put it inside a drawer, sat down and started to file a report.

Ranveer watched him, open-mouthed.

'But... but... but he's a beggar,' he protested. 'How—?'

Rahul smiled at him. 'This is the CBI, Ranveer, not a police station. We have many men working undercover,' he said.

I looked at the man in front of me, and wondered what to do. To be honest, when you imagine an incompetent cop you visualize one of those greasy, lazy, middle-aged morons who live off bribes and scaring local vendors. Yeah, there were innumerable such cops, and I could see *them* being taken for a ride. But this guy came as a surprise. For one, he was young, maybe just touching thirty. Also, he looked energetic, alert and more importantly, he didn't *look* the gullible sort. To fool someone like this meant the gang was really good. I could feel the beginning of the chase stirring in my mind.

But part of me was still utterly contemptuous of PSI Ranveer Singh of the Delhi Police. The man was an idiot, this half of me said, it was obvious. He had taken part in a fictitious raid and hadn't even known that he was being taken for a ride.

The other part of me felt sorry for the guy. He was young, he was ambitious, and above all, he seemed to be eager to serve the law. Also, he had walked into trouble he couldn't have anticipated.

Screw it. I'd been in enough messes in my life to know that a helping hand from above is always a good thing. Stops you from doubting yourself and your ability.

I leaned forward. 'So, Ranveer. What the hell happened to you, man?'

Ranveer looked up. He tried to smile, but what emerged was a lopsided grimace. 'I don't know, sir.'

'Well, we all do. You were taken for a ride like a mindless idiot, and you didn't even know it.'

Ranveer looked down, not meeting my eyes. I took pity on him.

'But then you don't look like a mindless idiot, so I'll give you the benefit of the doubt. Tell me what happened.'

Haltingly at first, and then speaking freely, Ranveer recounted everything that had happened, from the phone call to the raid to the realization they had been duped and the sinking feeling that he was done for.

When he fell silent, Rahul said, 'So there were four of them?'

Ranveer nodded.

I pushed his report across the table to him. 'This is yours?'

Another nod.

'You found this out?'

Nod.

'All on your own?'

Nod.

'Did anyone ask you to do this?'

'No, sir, it was me.' His face screwed up pleadingly. 'Sir, tell me, if you'd been in my place—'

'Kid,' I interrupted. 'If I'd been in your place, this mess wouldn't have happened. I didn't join the CBI to screw myself over.'

Ranveer hung his head again, and spoke in a low voice. 'I know what I've done, sir. You don't have to insult me for me to know that. I needed your help, which is why I came here. If you help me, we can sort this out quickly. But even if you refuse to help me, don't make the mistake of assuming that I'm giving up. I won't rest, sir. On my own, it'll take me much, much longer, but I'll get them in the end, sir. One way or another, I'll get them, I promise you that.'

He was getting worked up, but still speaking quietly, voice thick with emotion.

I smiled inwardly. I'd judged Ranveer accurately. Whatever he might be, he was definitely not a fool. Or a quitter.

'Calm down, Ranveer,' I said. 'You said exactly what I wanted to hear. Of course we'll help you.'

A look of gratitude spread across his face. 'Thank you, sir!' he said.

I passed over his report to Rahul. 'I want you to coordinate with these police stations. These are the only cases that have been registered. Speak with all of them, talk to the IOs handling the cases, talk to the man who took down the complaint. They may know something we can use. Ranveer, you'll go through all the records we have. You're the only one who saw those four men. Let's hope there are some police records for at least one of them.'

The beggar was looking at me expectantly. 'Shankar, you get on the phone with Minister Gupta. We'll need to talk to him.'

Ranveer interrupted. 'But, sir, he's refusing to talk!'

'He'll talk to me.'

Another thought struck me. I turned to a full-bearded sadhu who was dozing on a nearby desk, his feet on the table. 'Mohan!'

The sadhu snapped to attention. 'Yes, sir!'

'Get the sketch artist. Get him to talk to Ranveer and draw up descriptions. I want everything double time. These men have duped the police long enough. But now they're up against us. They won't get far.'

Shankar had gotten on the phone immediately. He now turned to me. 'Sir, Gupta's PA on the line. He's being... uncooperative.'

'Looks like he needs another slap, this time from the real CBI,' I muttered and picked up the phone.

'Waseem Khan. CBI Deputy Commissioner, Special Investigations. Who is this?'

'Myself Chauhan, Mantriji's PA. We won't speak to anyone. We—'

'Chauhan saab, if you want to be thrown in jail for obstructing the CBI's investigations, *please* say so. There's a cell here I'm itching to fill.'

'But—'

'No buts. Jail or home. You decide.'

Silence.

'Good. I'll be there tomorrow at ten. Tell your boss to be ready,' I said and hung up.

I turned back to Ranveer and saw he was looking slightly awed. 'Don't worry, kid,' I said kindly. 'You're working with the CBI now. We'll get them. You'll have your revenge soon.'

Ranveer looked exactly like Akbar did when he got his Gems.

The chase was on.

5

Birth of a Con

His experience had scarred him. His dream, his passion, the essential meaning of his very existence had been shattered. For weeks, Ajay walked around in a stupor, not caring, not feeling anything but a dumb numbness. Seeing his son broken had mended something inside his father, and he got up and started to live a little; if anything, to get the boy going again. Soon, he found Ajay a job at a local car mechanic's garage in the Fort area.

It was while he was hammering a hole into the chassis of a Premier Padmini that enlightenment came to Ajay.

If the law didn't want him, maybe the other side would.

When it comes to doing anything unlawful, there are hundreds of ways to get it wrong, but only one way to do it right. It was that simple. You just had to figure out the one right way.

A couple of weeks into the job at the garage, Ajay had already caught the owner's eye for his exceptional intelligence, which the man felt was clearly being wasted. Finally, one day, Albert Pinto called Ajay into the office at the back of the garage.

'Tell me something, Ajay,' he said, when Ajay had settled into the seat in front of him with a mug of tea and a breadroll. 'I've been asking around about you, and I heard that you're some kind of scholar. Is that true?'

Ajay didn't say anything, just shrugged.

'You don't talk much, either. I've heard the others say you're a loner. Is *that* true?'

Ajay just stared back.

'Well, your father said you'd be a good worker, and I guess I can't complain. But if you have a head for numbers, I have another role for you, if you're interested.'

'What is it?'

'Manage my accounts. I can't do math to save my life, and you're good with numbers, right?'

Ajay nodded. The first hatchings of a plan had already begun to form in his mind.

'Well then, it's settled. You'll be working in the office outside my cabin,' Pinto said, and leaned forward. 'But don't get any ideas, son. I may not be as smart as you are, but I know very well how to make people hurt. If I find anything wrong, you'll be sorry I trusted you.'

Ajay stared back blankly. This, however, seemed to satisfy Pinto, and he started work as the accountant for the garage.

His days were dreary, mundane. The drudgery began at eight in the morning; Ajay was the first person in. Through the day, they would all see him in the office, sweating over sheaves of paper. Some contained pages of numbers and tables and data, others contained tax workouts, and some, if anyone were to notice, looked suspiciously like long profiles of people. Had Pinto tried to find out what they were, he would have been surprised to know that they were all amateur dossiers on failed police aspirants who could now be found across the city, engaged in menial jobs. The one place Pinto never ventured near was Ajay's desk – it was too cluttered with papers containing important-looking figures.

Lunch was a boisterous community affair at the run-down roadside stall behind the garage. Other than that, there was not much of a break. By the time the clock struck ten, everyone left, including the manager. Then, it was left to Ajay to stash all the important documents away, lock up the garage and go home. Once a week, he took all the money the garage made and deposited it in the bank, keeping aside enough for the workers' wages.

Pinto had warned him of the possibility of being waylaid on the way home, by the usual goons wanting to make a quick buck. These were dangerous times, with the Bombay mafia's rising clout. But for some reason, Ajay never got into trouble. Just the one time, he came to work with a black eye, but he refused to say anything about it, or how he'd got it. When Pinto checked, the money was all there in the bank.

'How do you do it, Ajay?' the workers would ask. He would smile, but never explain.

In December that year, after Ajay had spent nearly six months as the garage accountant, Pinto called him into his office and told him he wouldn't be around for a week or so.

'It's my niece's wedding, I have to be there. I'm leaving you in charge.'

Ajay shook his head. 'The others won't like it. I've been here only a few months.'

'Well, for all purposes, Jairam will be the boss. But true power lies wherever the money is, remember that,' Pinto said, nodding sagely.

Power lies wherever the money is. In a million possible futures, the sentence went by unnoticed.

Ajay would turn down the offer.

Pinto would give the job to someone else.

Ajay would live out most of his life planning to quit the garage.

In all those million possible futures, this would be a very short book.

But here, and now, the words hit Ajay. True power lies wherever the money is. Suddenly, his future clicked into place. That was it! The nascent plan that Ajay had been turning over in his mind suddenly took shape. Here was the one corner piece that would make sense of this jigsaw puzzle.

Pinto was still speaking. 'So it doesn't matter, the men know you'll be in charge anyway, and it's not as if they don't like you or anything. Are you going to eat that?' He pointed at the bun maska Ajay had been munching on when he came in.

Ajay snapped back to reality. 'Huh? Oh no, please take it. Sure you won't need anyone else to mind the place while you're gone?'

'No, no,' Pinto said, mid-chomp. 'You guys can handle it, I know.'

That night, Ajay re-examined the rules.

He wanted money, because he knew it would get him power, the kind that lets you order cops around. And maybe, just maybe, with that money, he might be able to make a difference. And here it was, the opportunity, on a silver platter that had Albert Pinto written all over it. It would be easy to take the money and feed him some bullshit about thugs mugging him when they knew his boss wasn't around. Oh, it would be so damn easy, Ajay could hardly believe it.

On the other hand, this was exactly what he despised. This greed, this immorality was what had got him here in the first place; it was what had destroyed his dream in one fell blow, that conversation with two fallen cops. Would he turn into the same kind of person who wrecked someone else's life just to get rich? Money should be for the people. It should be used to *help*, not destroy.

There was also the fact that Pinto was himself not a wealthy man. He ran a garage, he was a man of limited resources and skills; if Ajay broke him, he would not be able to recover. Could Ajay really do that to him? Had he changed that much? From aspiring lawman to hardened outlaw, was this him?

It was the longest night Ajay spent, but at the end of it, he made a decision. It would shape his life, his future, indeed, his very existence.

He *would* get the money, and he *would* get the power. But certainly not by stealing from a trustful garage owner.

Ajay arrived at the garage the next morning, lighter in head and heart and finally with a purpose, although he still didn't know how he would achieve his new goals.

But destiny is a funny thing. You spend all your life waiting for it to change everything, and then you turn your back for just a minute and it comes and kicks you in the unmentionables. Ajay had no idea, but the change he was yearning for was about to begin its workings that very day.

At around noon, just as Ajay was finishing up with a set of records, Jairam lumbered into the office, followed by a large man bearing a briefcase and a red handkerchief with which he mopped his forehead. It was cool in Bombay's December, but he still managed to sweat.

'Ajay, this is P.K. Sharma. Pinto sir has sent him to keep an eye on... us... till he comes back,' Jairam spat at Ajay, the pause on the 'us' making it obvious that he felt the supervision was designed solely for Ajay.

'Sir, please have a seat. Would you like some tea or sherbet?' Jairam said, fawning.

Sharma flopped into Pinto's seat behind the office's main desk and nodded at Jairam. 'Thanks, a cup of tea would be great.'

Jairam turned to Ajay, who stared back pokerfaced, firmly settled in his chair. Jairam now looked iffy about his own suggestion. It meant that he would have to leave the new man in charge with Ajay, and *he* had wanted to be the one to show the boss the ropes. Now, he'd pretty much shot himself in the foot.

Grumbling at himself, Jairam stomped out, and they could hear him yelling at the nearest man in his path.

'So, Ajay! What do you do, exactly?' Sharma said, the red handkerchief now slowly being reduced to a rag with every wipe.

'I'm the accountant. I keep the books,' Ajay said. 'So you're looking in for Mr Pinto?'

'Yes, yes I am. He'll be gone a week or so, told me to look in on you all from time to time,' Sharma said.

'That's great, thanks. So how do you know Mr Pinto?'

Pat came the answer. 'Oh, we're neighbours. Known each other since we were kids.'

Ajay's brow creased. Something was not right here, and he tilted his head to one side as if trying to remember something. 'You live near his place?'

'Yeah. I'm coming from there right now.'

Ajay's face cleared as the memory forced its way through. 'Good, good, that's a good locality. Nice shoes, by the way.'

Sharma looked baffled, and peered down at his worn-out pair, trying and failing to figure out how the description fit. 'Huh? These, really?'

'Yeah, really,' Ajay said, and smiled. 'They look like they've been really well used.'

'Oh, right, right…' Sharma trailed off. 'Ah, there's the tea!'

A ragamuffin strolled in with a couple of minuscule cups without saucers, plonked them on the table and walked out.

Sharma looked relieved. For his part, he was beginning to think something was off about Ajay. For one, he didn't look remotely like someone working in a garage, he looked much too frail and scholarly. Then there was the way the kid spoke, in that voice.

As he sipped his tea, Sharma stole a glance at Ajay, and caught him staring right back at him. It was a disconcerting gaze, calculated to unsettle Sharma.

Sharma pottered around for another hour or so and then left, mumbling something about needing to be somewhere else and promising he'd be back tomorrow. He hadn't been prepared for this. He would be tomorrow, though.

That night, Sharma sat with his gang of three men and went through the plan again, step by step. So Pinto had left, put a moron and a kid in charge. The moron was not a problem, but the kid was. Looked like he knew too much, and Sharma did not like it. Nobody intimidated him! And he hated to admit it, but without saying a single word out of place or spewing any threats, the puny runt had stood in front of the massively built Sharma and been totally at ease, actually throwing the older man off. He couldn't allow that to happen again.

Over the next week, Sharma spent a lot of time in the office, yelling at people, chatting up customers, being the generally genial boss everyone wants. Ajay hardly paid him any attention, choosing to stay buried in his papers. He even took a day off, something he hadn't done since he started working at the garage. Slowly, Sharma's worries dissipated, and he told himself he had been worrying for no reason. Besides, how could a scrawny kid who only knew how to do numbers mess things up at all?

Four days later, it was bank day. Ajay left the garage at the usual time and following the usual route, with the bag in which he usually carried the money. Sharma's men were all in place, and they watched as Ajay walked straight into the trap.

The young man turned into a small lane off the street when he found himself cornered against a lamppost by three burly men who had just detached themselves from the surroundings. It was almost noon and there were lots of people around, but these men seemed oblivious, intent only on Ajay's scared face and trembling bag.

One of them spoke quietly. 'Just drop the bag, boy. Drop it and walk away, without any fuss.' As he spoke, a switchblade knife slid into his hand. So did two more in the others' hands.

Ajay's eyes darted from one man to another. They all looked the same, meaning that none of them was interested in him, just the bag he was carrying. Which in turn meant they probably wouldn't kill him if he dropped it and ran. It also meant they would definitely kill him if he didn't.

A low whistle to his right made him look around. Sharma was standing there, leaning against the side of a shop, smoking a cigarette and watching the scene. Their eyes met.

Sharma dropped the cigarette, crushed it

under his shoe with exaggerated care and, not looking away, shook his head slowly. Give him the bag and run away, his eyes said. That way, you'll live.

With a whimper, Ajay dropped the bag and started backing away. The first man reached down and grabbed the bag, nodded to the others and walked away. Sharma walked up to Ajay and spoke kindly. 'Don't worry. We won't kill you. You don't say anything about us, and we can keep it that way. Got it?'

Ajay nodded, his face a mask of fright. But he was trying to say something. 'P-p-p-please, Sharmaji. P-p-p-please take m-m-me with you,' he stammered.

Surprised, Sharma asked, 'What did you say?'

'Take me with you, Sharmaji. Teach me what you do! I want to learn!' Ajay said a little more confidently.

'You want to be a conman?' Sharma said incredulously. 'You, the scholar? Why?'

'I want money, Sharmaji.'

'Money? Well, at least you're honest enough to admit that.' Sharmaji looked around. 'I'll think about it. Now fuck off.'

He started to walk away, but Ajay clung

to his arm. 'How? Sharmaji? When will I see you?'

Sharmaji shook his hand free. 'Soon. I'll find you. Now go away.' He walked briskly to the corner, gave a small wave, and disappeared.

Ajay didn't return to the garage. Instead, he went home and waited. When the clock struck eleven, he put on his clothes and went out into the night.

Outside the shady, run-down shack, a sign read 'Double Without Trouble'. Inside, Sharma was sitting on his makeshift throne. He was an elated man tonight. He had just made a fortune from a robbery that had gone off without a hitch. And he would use the money for a con he'd set up just a week ago. He had been luring people in, promising to double their money if they invested in him. The first time, he gave them double the amount they'd invested. Naturally, this caused quite a flutter, and the next time, they brought more money, and more people with more money. The second time too, they would get double the amount they'd given him. Just think of what they would bring the third time! Sharma chuckled to think of all those people who would soon be disappointed. The good, old-fashioned con game had worked twice before and there was no reason why it would not work again.

The goons he'd hired had just delivered the bag to him, taken their cut and left. He'd not even had time to open the bag to count how much he'd made when his visitors started coming in. Well, it didn't matter. There was certainly more in it than what these guys needed to be paid. He would use the rest of the money to do something really extravagant this time.

One by one, the men came, handed Sharma their money, exchanged some small talk and left. He'd already kept some wads of cash on the table, just enough to dispel doubts. He kept paying the 'doubled investment', holding off from opening the bag as long as he could. The less people who saw the amount of cash in that bag the better.

Sharma had just gotten rid of a most annoying specimen, and beckoned to the next in line. The man was slight, in a shirt and bellbottoms and with a cap pulled down low over his face. 'So, how much will it be, son?' Sharma said, pulling out an official-looking form.

'All of it, Sharmaji,' said Ajay.

Years of conning and playing people pitched in all at once and fought a fierce micro-second-long battle with Sharma's reflexes, which at that point were already activating his vocal chords to emit a full-throated scream. The years won.

Sharma fought back the scream and said, 'You! How—'

Ajay sat down in the chair opposite Sharma. 'That's not important, Sharmaji. What's important is that I'm here. What can you give me?'

'I see. You want to join me—'

'Not really,' interrupted Ajay. 'I want *you* to join *me*.'

Sharma raised his eyebrows; he had fully recovered from the shock of half a minute ago. The impudence of the boy! 'Do you know what you're talking about, *boy*? Just because you found me running this business, you think you can—'

'Oh, I've done a lot more than that, Sharmaji,' said Ajay, settling into his chair with a cocksure smile. 'Why don't you check that bag?'

'What?'

'Check the bag you stole from me, Sharmaji.'

Suddenly, Sharmaji wasn't sure any more. With mounting dread, he unzipped the bag. What he saw nearly made his heart stop.

It was filled with wads of paper, each cut in the size of a ten-rupee note.

Thunderstruck, he looked up to see Ajay watching him. 'How—'

'Simple. I let you believe you were fooling me.'

This was when anyone would begin to get angry, and Ajay knew it. He leaned forward and spoke softly. 'Listen to me. Nobody here knows what's actually in that bag. I could tell them, and they could then decide what to do with you. I'm sure you can imagine what kind of future *that* entails. But agree to work with me, and we can forget this whole thing.'

Sharmaji realized the trickiness of the situation. There really was no way out. 'Why do you think I would work with you, you little son of a—'

'Because, Sharmaji, I can make you rich. What you're doing now will only get you small-time money and really big-time enemies, and not just a few. All of these men you're conning will be after you. I'll make sure that we make very few enemies and a whole lot of money. What do you say?'

Sharmaji opened his mouth, then shut it again.

Half an hour later, he and Ajay were sitting at a tea shop, sipping on piping–hot tea. He was still trying to figure Ajay out.

'You meant what you said back there?' he asked.

'Of course.'

'Because, you know, I've known a lot of people who claimed to be able to do a lot of things. Most of them are in jail. The rest are dead.'

'Well, I have the plan, Sharmaji. I don't have the resources yet, which is where you come in. I was hoping you would let me in on some of the cons going around.'

'I see. Well, your plan was good, I must say, Ajay. To come up with this plan in a couple of days—'

Ajay coughed. 'Actually, it was before that.'

'Before? Since when?'

Ajay looked sheepish now. 'Since you walked into the garage that first day.'

Sharmaji was so surprised that he stood right up, his mouth agape. 'Since then? You've been planning this since then?' he cried.

'Calm down, Sharmaji! Calm down. Please sit,' Ajay said consolingly.

Miffed, the older man sat back down. 'I want to know how.'

Ajay started to protest, but saw the look on Sharmaji's face and decided against it. 'I realized you were a conman the day I saw you. There was obviously nothing in the garage you could want, otherwise you'd have been chatting up Jairam. So it had to be the money. That money only went out on one day of the week. It would be with me. So…' Ajay trailed off.

A note of grudging respect crept into Sharmaji's voice. 'So you planned this whole thing from then? The mugging, which *I* did, coming to my place of business, threatening me — all this was to get my attention?'

Ajay nodded.

Sharmaji was vastly impressed. To con a conman was a difficult thing, but to do it when you're hardly out of your teens, and in such a manner… it was bloody genius!

But there was something else Sharmaji was itching to know. 'How did you discover what my business was?'

Ajay smiled. 'From your shoes,' he replied.

'My—my shoes?' Sharmaji said, bewildered.

'Yes. I noticed you'd trodden in dung. And when you came into the office, it was still fresh. There's a cattle shed near here, and on the day I took a holiday I went there in disguise and saw you, and I put two and two together.'

It was simple, once he'd described it. But then…

'How did you know I was not a friend of Albert Pinto?'

Ajay grinned. 'Your shoes.'

'Oh, come on! Not the shoes again!'

'It's true. Look. There's a construction site at the mouth of Mr Pinto's lane. Anyone living on that lane would end up with a fine layer of white dust on their shoes. The boss came in like that every morning. But yours were clean, except for the dung.'

Sharmaji let out a long pent-up breath, and held up his glass of tea. 'Ajay, you're good. I've never met someone who can plan so far ahead.'

Ajay smiled again. 'Thank you. But there are a few more things we have to do before we can really start anything.'

'Oh?' said Sharmaji. 'What's that?'

'We have to get more people.'

Ajay had found a reason to persevere, even if this was a twisted version of his original plan. And he'd found a friend.

6

Wrong Man, Right Girl

Bimal Agarwal was a workaholic and a highly punctual man. His employees could correct their watches against his 11 a.m. arrival in office, daily without fail. A self-made man, Bimal Agarwal was born poor and had learnt the principles of life along the way. By sheer hard work and equally vital dollops of luck, he had managed to become a millionaire. Now, he was listed among the largest importers of ball bearings in the city.

His employees greeted him enthusiastically as always when he walked in this morning, and he casually nodded in return. He sat down at his desk, and dialled a number on his intercom.

'When is the next shipment arriving?' he asked, pen in hand.

He nodded, and jotted down details in a notepad.

'Okay, thanks,' he said and put the receiver down.

He called three employees and issued instructions for proper handling and receipt of the cargo, telling them that if need be, they were to grease the palms of the customs officers. The men nodded, and went back into the storeroom.

Agarwal made some rough calculations on paper, and smiled to himself. Knowing that he was about to hit the jackpot always made him smile. He took his glasses off and dabbed at his face with a handkerchief. He then got up and went to a locker and opened it. He took some cash out of his briefcase and placed it systematically inside. He slammed the metal door shut and locked it, just as he registered three people walking into his office out of the corner of his eye.

'Good morning, sir.' said the Sardar, curtly. 'I am Harpal Singh, from the Central Bureau of Investigation.'

He held up an ID in his right hand, to let Agarwal confirm this.

The old man was taken aback, and beads of sweat appeared on his bald pate. He took a few seconds to regain his composure.

'W-what is this about?' he asked politely.

'We have gathered intelligence that you have been making illegal transactions and also dabble in hawala funding,' the Sardar said.

'I don't understand,' Agarwal said.

'Black money, unaccounted cash,' Singh said matter-of-factly. 'Understand now?'

'This is ridiculous!' Agarwal yelled.

The third officer held a warrant right in front of his face. 'We have been ordered to confiscate all your liquid assets,' he said, twirling his moustache.

Agarwal stood his ground silently for a few seconds.

'Sir, you have to be cooperative if you want us to be unbiased in our investigation.'

Agarwal walked towards the locker resignedly. The officers emptied all the money, amounting to five lakh rupees, into the various suitcases they had with them.

'If you're cleared, the money will be returned,' Singh said as he slammed the door and made his way out.

The three of them grinned victoriously at each other and quickly got into their cars, before they rid themselves of their fake beards and moustaches. They had triumphed again, these Robin Hoods, stealing from the rich to give to the poor.

Ajay beamed. He asked his partners, Joginder, Iqbal and Sharmaji, to meet him later; he had to rush to Regal Cinema at Colaba for a show of *Top Gun*. Priya would be waiting for him.

It had been several years since he had begun courting Priya. But he had never seen her so stuck on one request for so long.

He hadn't been able to pay much attention to the movie that everyone was raving about. Tom Cruise, the new Hollywood superstar, was taking the world by storm. He looked so handsome that Ajay finally conceded he had seen a star who was better looking than him.

They were walking near the Gateway of India with popcorn in their hands.

'What's the matter, Ajay?' Priya asked, looking at his frowning face. 'Didn't like the movie?'

'Loved it. What about you? Did you like the movie, or just Tom Cruise?' he said, with a wink.

'Just Tom Cruise,' she giggled. 'But what's the matter? You've been rather morose all evening.'

'It's nothing, Priya.'

She nodded and looked away. He knew that she knew something was wrong. It had been like this since their college days. Ever since they had graduated from Chetna College in 1979, they had been besotted with each other, these past seven years.

'Okay,' he mumbled. 'I was just wondering what it would be like to be rich. You know? Tom Cruise-rich. As rich as, maybe even, your father.'

'You've never met my father,' she muttered. 'How do you know he's rich?'

'Because of the way you carry yourself. Such poise, such elegance. Not to mention the jewellery.'

'Listen, Ajay,' she said, looking at him wide-eyed. 'I like you for who you are. Such thoughts change a man. Just work hard and the world will be at your feet.'

He looked at her and smiled. They continued to walk in the direction of her house.

Ajay's thoughts drifted in another direction: for as long as there have been people making money, there have been people waiting to take it from them, he mused. History is rife with swindlers and brazen impostors who have used the trust of other to propel them to fame and riches. He himself was one such con-artist.

Well, he wasn't one yet. He was more of a low-level conman for now. He'd soon be one of the biggest con-artists in history though, he thought. And there was no harm in taking money away from crooks, he rationalized.

'When are you coming to see dad?' Finally, it was out.

Ajay realized there was no point in stalling any further.

'Tomorrow?'

Priya could not believe it. 'Oh, really? Please come in the morning then, before he leaves for office.'

Arriving at the posh locality of D' Monte Park in Bandra next morning, Ajay waited for fifteen minutes on the porch of Priya's building. The plan was to meet her dad and then to whisk her away for a romantic day together.

Priya stepped out just then, and he grinned at her. She didn't reciprocate his enthusiasm, smiling feebly as she approached him.

'Daddy wants to meet you. He's coming down.'

'Sooner or later he has to meet his son-in-law to be.' Ajay smiled at her.

And then Ajay saw her father. He froze. The same bald pate on a grim face. Only yesterday the man had been Ajay's victim. Thankfully, Ajay had been in disguise as a sardar, covered up in a turban and with a full beard to boot.

It was Bimal Agarwal. Of all the Agarwals in India, it had to be this one who had decided to be Priya's father. Damn.

Bimal Agarwal walked straight towards the couple.

'Daddy, this is Ajay,' Priya said brightly.

The man nodded. Ajay managed to muster up a smile. The old man didn't seem impressed.

'So what do you do, Ajay?'

Ajay didn't say anything. He wasn't in any shape to think straight. Bimal Agarwal repeated his question.

'Um-uh, nothing, sir. Looking for a job,' was all Ajay could say.

'Well, better get one. It's difficult to sustain oneself in today's world,' was Agarwal's fatherly advice. 'Anyway, I do have work. Unlike the two of you, still behaving like carefree teenagers.'

He walked away from the young couple. Ajay disliked the man already. He felt a perverse pleasure in knowing that he, a 'carefree teenager', had robbed this man of his earnings. At the same time, he felt a sudden wave of guilt. He had just robbed from the love of his life. Well, indirectly.

'Don't pay any heed. He's been in a bad mood since yesterday. Apparently, the CBI confiscated five lakh rupees for some investigation. He's been crabby ever since.'

Later that evening, though, Mr Bimal Agarwal's mood lightened. One of the officers – not the Sardar – paid him a visit to return the 'confiscated' money. He smiled as he heard that he had been cleared by the CBI. And so, things settled and Ajay grew comfortable dating Priya. The weeks turned to months and the months became a year. Ajay was in a much better financial position now. But Priya was always apprehensive of losing him.

Today, Ajay had brought her to Sanjay Gandhi National Park. They walked through the woods, like all the other couples making a slow promenade through the greenery.

But it seemed Priya had something on her mind, and when she was sure there was nobody else around, she brought it up. 'Ajay, you're never around.' They were sitting on a small bench beside a pond.

Ajay's arm was around Priya, her head resting on his shoulder.

'I know, sweetie. There's just too much work, you know.'

'But, you've never told me. What do you do, exactly?'

She could feel him stiffen. 'Priya, don't ask me,' he said woodenly. 'I promise you that my work will never hurt anyone who shouldn't be hurt. That's all.'

She sighed. 'You have so many secrets, Ajay. I love you, but sometimes I feel I hardly know you. That's not the way I want to live my life, tiptoeing around your secrets.'

'You know you don't have to, Priya. Tell you what,' he said, turning to her and taking her small hand in his. 'I'll tell you everything. Everything you want to know. But not now. Give me a little more time, and you'll know all my secrets. Promise.'

He meant every word, and he knew she believed him. But he saw sadness lurking in her eyes.

'What is it?' he asked, concerned for the first time.

She shook her head. 'It's nothing.'

Ajay lifted her chin gently with one hand. Her skin was white in the moonlight, pale as winter, and her eyes were large and brimming. 'Priya, this is me you're talking to. You know I'll know when you're not telling me something. What is it?'

She turned away, her hand still in his. 'This can't go on forever, Ajay.'

There was more, he knew it. He stayed silent, waiting.

In a low voice, she said, 'Papa has found a boy.'

Ajay relaxed. 'That's it?' He laughed. 'Don't you worry about that. These things take time, and you never know what will happen meanwhile.'

Priya dropped the bomb. 'He's fixed the date for the engagement.'

She looked up at him, and saw him staring into space, his face expressionless.

'Did you hear what I said, Ajay? I'm going to be engaged in three months!' she said incredulously.

'I heard you, darling, I heard. Three months?' He smiled. 'That's a long time.'

She shook her head. 'No, Ajay, it isn't. You won't even know when it's gone by.'

He turned to face her. 'I just have one question. Do you like the fellow?'

Her eyes widened. 'Like? How dare you ask me that? How can you even think—'

'No, no, don't get me wrong,' he said soothingly. 'What I meant was, have you seen him? Do you know him?'

She shook her head, her arms folded across her chest, the picture of hurt indignation.

'Good. Then you have nothing to worry about.' He drew her closer to him. 'Listen to me. You won't marry him. I know that. But will you marry me?'

She gasped, even angrier. 'Really? So that's how you're going to propose to me? Wow, you're a romantic!' She looked as if she was on the verge of flouncing off.

He shook his head. 'No, I'm not proposing. Believe me, when I propose, you'll know it. I'm only asking you. Would you marry me?'

'Not right now, I wouldn't!'

'Come on, Priya. Set your anger aside for just a minute. Would you?'

She softened. 'Of course I would, you idiot.'

He smiled. 'Then here's my promise. You won't marry him. Nobody will take you from me.'

She looked worried. 'Ajay, you didn't hear what I said. I don't know what you do, where you go—'

'I'll tell you everything, Priya,' he interrupted her. 'Everything. But not now. There are a few more things I've got to do. And there is one big job I have to finish. I wish I could tell you all about it now, but I can't. I'm asking you to trust me.'

'Of course I trust you, Ajay! But won't you tell me something at least?'

'Priya, you're the most intelligent woman I know,' said Ajay, leaning back. 'Take a guess.'

She looked at him carefully. In a wary voice, she said, 'I don't know. But I don't think it's legal.'

Ajay smiled again. 'It isn't.'

She sighed again. 'I thought so. I think you're some kind of fancy thief. You're not stupid enough to be into petty thieving, and you actually have principles and ethics, so you can't be a murderer.'

Ajay watched her, smiling. 'Go on.'

'I also think you have some sort of strategy, and that you have a larger purpose in mind. I don't know what that is,' she finished.

Ajay nodded. 'You know, in college there were so many girls who had so much. But not one of them had brains like you.'

Her eyes danced mischievously. 'Girls? What, you're a chauvinist now?'

Ajay suddenly grew serious. 'Priya, I won't tell you anything yet. Not now. But like I told you before, I never hurt anyone who didn't deserve to be hurt. You know me, you know my principles, what I believe, what I stand for. You know I would never do anything to hurt the innocent.'

He watched her think. It was the longest thirty seconds of his life. Then she nodded.

'Yes, I do know you.'

'That's why I'm asking you to trust me. There are a few more things I have to wrap up, and then I'll be with you. Always. And wherever I go, you'll come with me.'

She chuckled. 'Boy, you're really corny, you know that?'

The danger had passed. Ajay realized that he had been holding his breath, and he let it go now in a whoosh of relief.

'Yeah, yeah, I guess so.'

She pressed against him again. 'So what do we do?'

His mind had started racing again. 'Do? We do nothing. Just keep doing whatever the hell your father says. But wait for me. I'll come for you before you get engaged.'

'Mmm. I wish Papa could see what I see in you,' she said wistfully. 'Then we wouldn't have these stupid complications.'

'Me too, Priya. But I'll win him over someday.'

'Win him over,' said Priya, surprised. 'How exactly?'

'I don't know yet. But I'll think of something.'

She was silent for a while, and he sensed her next question even as she spoke. 'Ajay, just tell me this. Your work. Why do you do it?'

'Why indeed,' he said playfully. 'I can't do anything else. My mind is always thinking, planning. And you're my muse.'

She looked up at him, soft, gentle and trusting, and he thought his heart would explode with love.

'You know,' she said softly, her slender fingers playing with his collar. 'You really can be very corny!'

Ajay smiled.

7

Cops and Cons

'So they suspended you?'

'Of course they did, sir. Wouldn't you have?'

Ranveer, Rahul and I were sitting in a restaurant next to the CBI office. It was a place all our officers frequented, we could speak freely there. A lot of power was concentrated in this room – they said more deals and tip-offs passed through here than in the building next door.

It was of course predictable, the way they had kicked Ranveer and his team out, suspending them after the raid at the minister's house. And it had happened the very next day.

'You see, sir,' Ranveer told us, sipping his tea, 'when I realized what had happened, I immediately contacted my superior. The next day, Shanti and I were summoned to Minister Gupta's bungalow.'

'Was your additional commissioner there?' I asked.

'Yes, sir. How did you know?' Ranveer asked, impressed by my omniscience.

I gestured for him to carry on. Some things you can't explain, you learnt through experience, and then hope all that experience will get you somewhere.

'Well, Minister Gupta refused to lodge an FIR.'

'Obviously. If he lodges an FIR, he has to disclose exactly what was stolen. He does that, he has to go back to Bihar to his cattle.'

'That's exactly what he said! We tried to explain to him that the police wouldn't be able to do anything if he did not lodge an FIR, but there was no way we could convince him. And he wouldn't rest until Shanti and I were suspended, in front of him.' Ranveer stopped, and I could see him battling with his humiliation.

It was the day after I had been assigned the case. Ranveer, Rahul and I had met at the restaurant at nine in the morning at my behest – I wasn't about to land up at the minister's residence with a nervous Ranveer in tow. I had to get him to relax more and worry less, especially since he had good reason to be apprehensive: the minister would most certainly throw a fit when he saw that despite the suspension, Ranveer was still on the case.

It helped. As Rahul and I spoke to him and drew him out, his inhibitions fell away through the binding power of shared experience.

'All right, Ranveer. It's time to face your demons,' I said, getting up and depositing a few coins on the table for our tea. 'We'd better leave now if we have to reach Gupta's place by ten.'

In a moment, Ranveer's face turned ashen again. 'You want me to come, sir? But why? Won't that just anger him further? He might—'

'He won't do anything, believe me,' I interrupted. 'You're with the CBI now. Don't forget that.'

I couldn't figure out the fellow. He was enterprising enough to gather all that evidence on the gang even after he had been suspended and then to approach the CBI, but on the other hand, he was frightened about what he didn't have to be frightened of. It was a strange dichotomy.

At exactly 10 a.m., the three of us arrived at Minister Gupta's bungalow. Rahul stayed back in the jeep while Ranveer and I went to keep our appointment. Our approach was completely unhindered – the men at the gate stood aside respectfully, the other guards strolling about on the lawn steered clear of us. It was pretty obvious that the fellow didn't want to antagonize the law in any way. Well, not so soon, at any rate.

A puny, bespectacled man whom I placed as Minister Gupta's PA – notorious after the infamous 'raid' – opened the door for us with an almighty scowl on his face, which deepened when he saw Ranveer. 'Come this way, please,' he snarled. Typical, I thought, power gone to his head. Well, if the gang had slapped him, at least they had done *one* thing right.

The PA led the way to a room on the right,

which would typically have been the library of a bungalow such as this, but instead was filled with trophies and heads of prey. 'The police are here, sir,' he announced.

For a moment, it felt like I was in a scene from a badly made mobster movie, in which the minister was presenting himself as the omnipotent mafia boss. Reclining in a mammoth armchair behind an ornate, garish table, the minister gestured for us to come in with a pudgy hand covered with rings and bracelets.

'I've already spoken to the police,' he said, affecting a boredom that was at odds with the thin film of sweat visible on his forehead. He was scared shitless, and he reeked.

I decided to help nudge that emotion to the surface. Walking slowly up to the table, I leaned forward and deliberately placed my hands on the tabletop. With just enough of a pause to let him know that I was taking control of the situation, I said, as menacingly as possible, 'I am not the police. I am the CBI.'

At times like this, a rasping voice helps. And my voice rasped like nobody's business.

The illusion of calm shattered; his face crumpled. 'CBI? Again?'

'No, not again. For the first time. The men who looted you weren't from the CBI. I am. And you will talk to me.'

The man's eyes swivelled to Ranveer, filled with anger for a moment, then readjusted themselves when his brain realized that the man was with me.

Ranveer chose this moment to speak up. 'Sir, this is Waseem Khan. He's a big figure in the CBI. Waseem sir has decided to investigate your case.'

The minister panicked again. 'But-but-but I don't want to file an FIR! I've already told—'

'It's all right, you don't have to. And I'm investigating a bigger case, not your case alone,' I said, settling down in the seat across from the minister. Just to spite the man, I placed my feet on the table with exaggerated slowness, in my very own mafia movie. 'Don't make the mistake of thinking I'm a fool, minister. I know exactly why you're not lodging an FIR. I also know that you've told a few pals of yours, but they aren't helping out because they've got the same things to hide that were stolen from you. I know everything,' I said calmly, not taking my eyes off his. 'Minister,' I added.

He gestured to Ranveer. 'And him?'

'He's with me.'

'But-but it's because of that idiot that I was robbed in the first place! I thought he was suspended! Just you wait, I'll see to it that—'

I interrupted before he could get his bluster back. 'You won't see to anything. In fact, you should thank him, because he brought me into the game. Besides, I said he's with me.'

The man gave up at last. There was no way he could win, not even on his own turf. No matter how powerful you are, nothing beats two decades of experience of running after criminals and breaking them. And everyone knew I did it especially well.

I got up. 'I want you to show me everything. What they did, how they got in, where they searched, everything. No, not him…' He'd started pointing to the PA. 'I want *you* to come with me.'

I was thorough. Two hours' worth of thorough. By the time we left, I wouldn't have been surprised if the minister was seriously considering giving it all up and going back to his cattle.

On the way back to HQ, I got Ranveer to fill Rahul in on all that had happened. I was driving, and the steady intonation of his summary helped me concentrate.

I was only half listening, though. There were too many thoughts rattling around in my head, the foremost of which was the realization that this wouldn't be an easy case. The men were clearly professionals, and had thought of every single thing. I prided myself on noticing the little things that gave a criminal away, but these guys were good – I'd found nothing.

So, we would have to do this the hard way.

I interrupted Ranveer's narrative. 'When we get to HQ, I want you two to get cracking. Rahul, you're already speaking to the police stations, correct? Good. Get on to them again. Stay on their asses until they give you something. Ranveer, did you describe the men for the sketches? Okay. Hand out those sketches to a few others. I want you to go through all the files we have – criminals, thugs, gangsters, petty crooks, don't even leave out the chain snatchers. See if you can find a record of any of those four men.'

The next week was spent in hectic boredom. Hectic because not a moment was wasted; it was work, work, work all the way. And boring because if you sit looking at file after file after file, it tends to get highly monotonous.

But it wasn't, of course, all boring. If the police diaries were correct, and if all of these acts had been committed by the same gang, then it would *most certainly* not be an easy chase. My eyes widened as I looked at the list of all the places the gang had hit – Bangalore, Bombay, Calcutta, Delhi, Lucknow, Patna, Indore, Guwahati, Salem, Trivandrum, Vizag – you name the place, they had struck there. Initially, there were just too many cases to put a finger on it, but I'd been on the force long enough to know that if you looked hard enough, there was always an underlying pattern.

And soon, I found that pattern. The victims were always in that grey area between law-abiding and crooked, and the men were always masquerading as the law. Be it the CBI or the police or even the income-tax bastards in some places, these guys were making a mockery of the law, and something told me that it was deliberate. If they were good enough to get away with this, why did they constantly stick to one modus operandi? They should surely develop some other methods, because sooner or later, the police would catch on, and then their lucky streak would run out.

But no, it seemed that these guys were mocking the police, and there had to be a reason. Usually, these things were subconscious, but this was nothing like that, it was a major part of their strategy. Of course, it stood to reason that if they used another MO, they would be virtually impossible to track amid the sheer number and variety of criminals these days, and we couldn't have connected them to the other crimes in any case.

Suddenly, it clicked into place.

I looked to the next table, where Ranveer was poring over the old files the CBI maintained on criminals. He looked haggard, on the verge of dropping off. Time to wake the kid up with some adrenalin.

'Ranveer, wake up, man!'

With a jolt, he came around, and when he saw me, his eyes focused immediately. Maybe I did look a little excited.

'Find Mohan. Tell him to get you all the files we have on ex-cops. Go through them.'

'Ex-cops?' Ranveer said, uncomprehending. 'What about these, sir?'

'Leave them. First go through those files. I'll go home for a bit while you're at it.'

'Okay, sir.' Puzzled, he staggered off to find Mohan.

It had been three days since I'd gone home. As I parked the scooter, walked up the narrow stairs and unlocked the door, I shuddered to think what my wife was planning to do with me. The last time, she'd been explicitly threatening with regard to my entrails.

But I was lucky this time. Maybe it was because I'd told her this would get me a promotion and an increment, or maybe I was looking exhausted. Shazia took pity on me, and fed me the most delicious dinner I'd had in months. Akbar was asleep, and it was just the two of us. It helped to see the spark of desire in her eyes, as well. It would be a happy, fulfilling night, I thought.

Yes, Shazia would be her usual shy self, which she usually was until I took her to bed – when she turned into a near-insatiable, passionate goddess.

The bed was soft, and so was she, filled as we both were with a longing to make love like we'd never done before. She lay beside me in her nakedness, and I slipped under the sheets beside her, reached out and—

R-R-R-R-R-RING!

Bloody stupid phone! How the hell did it know to ring exactly when it shouldn't!

Leaving Shazia alone in the bed, I ran to the phone. 'Yes, hello?'

It was Ranveer, and he sounded excited. 'We've got him, sir! I found him!'

Lying with Shazia, the case had receded to the back of my mind. But Ranveer's voice brought it back. I hadn't really expected my hunch to bear results, and not so quickly, but now that it had, the puzzle immediately became a little clearer in my mind. 'Who is he?'

'P.K. Sharma, sir. Used to be a constable with the Chandigarh police, Sector 9 police station.'

'Used to be, huh? I'll be right in,' I said, and hung up.

I turned around, wondering how I'd tell Shazia, when I saw her standing at the door to the living room, the bedsheet wrapped around her, lightning in her eyes. Those last few words clearly hadn't gone down very well, it was apparent.

'Darling, I too want to—' I started, but she stopped me with a look and stalked back into the room, ignoring me.

Bloody hell.

I dressed hurriedly, apologized to Shazia again, who by this time was pointedly pretending to be asleep, started the scooter, yelled at a night-duty cop who was trying to stop me to question where the hell I was racing to at one at night, and was at my desk in less than twenty minutes.

'What've we got?'

From Ranveer's excited chatter and Rahul's calmer tones, I pieced together what they had found out. Ranveer's Sharmaji was a bent cop, but not fully crooked. He had been caught red-handed asking for a bribe of five thousand rupees from a local businessman. He said it was the first time he had tried to extort money, but it was actually his twenty-eighth, if all the cases lodged were to be believed. Apparently the man was trying to put together money for his second daughter's wedding, but he had chosen an ill-advised formula.

Sharma had been suspended in 1979, so he had eight years to hone his skills. By Ranveer's account, he was the man in charge, which meant that he had gathered at least three more men and formed a gang, then gone about looting the country's crooked.

'How did you know he'd be an ex-cop, sir?' said Ranveer. He was practically gushing now, seeming more in awe of me than ever.

'It's nothing, really. From your account of the raid, it was clear that the men knew exactly how to handle themselves, especially their leader. That means they must've had some experience, either raiding or being raided. It couldn't have been the second, because if you've been raided, your file is in our records. So it had to be the first. And who would have experience in raiding a place?'

'The police?' Ranveer finished.

'Exactly.'

It fit like a surgeon's hand in a latex glove. Disillusioned cop gets sacked, then gets back at the police by making them look like fools. It certainly fit.

But I sensed there was something not quite right with the theory, though. I couldn't put my finger on it.

'Give me a minute,' I told Ranveer. 'Something's not right here.'

'Not right? But you've got him, sir! We found him!'

I noticed Rahul nudge Ranveer into silence, and nodded my thanks at him.

Something was nagging me. I checked every detail in Sharma's file, and finally, the idea began to take shape.

From the file, Sharma came across as a simple, congenial sort with more children than cousins. He had been a high-school dropout, had just about been selected as a recruit for the police force, had a most unremarkable record in the force, and was dumb enough to get caught asking for a bribe the way he did. Whichever way I looked at it, I couldn't see this guy climbing out of that hole in his head where his brain ought to be and turn into a brilliant criminal mastermind overnight, not in five or eight or even a hundred years. To plan heists like this gang was doing required a certain level of genius, which was singularly lacking in Sharma's resume.

I looked up and shook my head. 'I think we're wrong. Call it a gut feeling, but Sharma is not the leader.'

'But sir, he was!' protested Ranveer. 'He was leading all the others throughout the raid, I know—'

'Maybe you're right, Ranveer. But I don't think he's the big fish. We'll go with it, of course, make him our prime suspect, but unofficially, I'm telling you. Keep your eyes open for more.'

Ranveer looked crestfallen. His big breakthrough had just been shot down, and I had to convince him it wasn't so. 'Listen to me, Ranveer. What you did was good. *You* got the breakthrough. *You* found Sharma. So cheer up. Even if it takes the investigation along a slightly different path, you should be happy.'

That was all I could manage before my self-consciousness about giving speeches kicked in, and taped my mouth shut.

I turned to Rahul. 'What do you have?'

Rahul was the most efficient man I knew, and he didn't disappoint now. Handing me a piece of paper, he said, 'That's his address. I activated my informers while Ranveer was phoning you. One of them got back to me.'

'Good. Anything else?'

'No, sir. But I also made Ranveer go through all known associates of Sharma. None of the three others have any records.'

Damn. That was a setback. But it was to be expected. In fact, it was more proof that Sharma couldn't be the brains behind the gang. It had to be someone else.

'Fine. Keep looking. There has to be something on the others. Find out whatever you can. And activate all your informers. Everyone you've got. It's time we nailed these suckers.'

All charged up, Rahul and Ranveer rushed out.

I sat back, not even remotely fired up. From the look of things, this wasn't going to be easy at all.

8

The Crazy Quartet

The sun was rising over the city, and the teeming millions were just awakening. The city that never sleeps, but does occasionally doze a little after downing a pint or two. But in this small bylane of Dongri, there were few who noticed the sunrise.

From his first-floor balcony, Ajay watched the figures as they scurried about, busy, wrapped up in their simple lives of work, pleasure and pain. They say every man is a unique, complex creature, but from where Ajay was standing, all of them seemed singularly indistinguishable from one another.

He stood there, lost in contemplation,

for a long time – a regular sight for the neighbourhood, which he did not realize. They'd all grown used to this odd little boy who kept to himself and his books; then the odd young man who stood stone-faced and dry-eyed as he watched his father's body being taken away to the funeral pyre; and then this odd, lanky man who still didn't say much but would often stand at his balcony for hours on end, staring into space.

He had been sixteen when his father had died, or rather, ceased to live: his will to get up and face another day had been eroded over the years into nothingness, until that night when he went to bed for the last time. At least it had been a peaceful death, but it was the final stamp of the orphan identity on Ajay.

Those who met Ajay didn't know what to make of him – a man who had an open face but eyes that were shuttered and an enigmatic smile. He was never discourteous, never loud, and kept to himself in a neighbourhood where everyone knew everything about everyone else. All his all-knowing, all-opining neighbours would be flummoxed if they were ever to attempt describing Ajay.

The jarring sound of the phone ringing behind him broke Ajay's train of thought. He strolled over unhurriedly and picked it up. It was Joginder.

'Hello, Ajay! Hello?' Joginder bellowed. He still had difficulty adjusting to the concept of a device with which he could hear someone hundreds of miles away. He'd almost died of joy when Ajay and Sharmaji had got him the telephone.

'I can hear you, Jogi, don't shout,' said Ajay. 'What news?'

'All quiet.'

'Anything in the papers?'

'Nope, nothing yet.'

'Checked everything?'

'Yes. Hindi, English, Punjabi, there's no mention of our—I mean—nothing anywhere.'

'Good. Sell off everything quickly before word gets out.'

'Will do.'

'See you at the wedding.'

'Okay.' Joginder paused, not knowing how to end the conversation. Ajay knew this, and helped by hanging up himself.

Several cities away, in old Delhi, Joginder went to the rear of his house and dumped the six newspapers he held into the lane behind. Then he went back inside and spent the next few minutes checking to ensure his conversation hadn't been overheard. His wife was fast asleep in their bedroom, and so were the fifteen others sleeping cramped in the hall of their two-room flat. Joginder tiptoed over the prostrate bodies and went out into the yard in front. In that run-down place, where everyone was absorbed in surviving from day to day, few had the time to notice a stick-thin youth picking up a couple of gunny bags and hurrying away.

Ajay knew Joginder would, in record time, get rid of everything they'd looted from the businessman in Delhi the previous evening. It had felt good too – the man was too cocky, too corrupt, and too careless. He'd been most cooperative, however, after a little P.K. Sharma bullying, and the loot was magnificent. Getting rid of it would've been a problem, but no need to worry there.

Sharmaji had chosen well when he'd picked out Joginder from a bunch of urchins a year or so ago. The kid had just managed to pick Ajay's pocket cleanly, and had almost got away before he had been accosted by a thick pair of arms and lifted clean off his feet. Sharmaji and Ajay had then taken Joginder to a local sweetmeats shop, explained to him that they had watched him pick four pockets before finally getting to Ajay, and told him that they could use his talents in their own operations. Initially, Joginder was to be just the handyman, the fellow who got rid of the booty without the cops getting wind of it, but soon, they realized the boy had brains, and more importantly, an earnest, open face that belied an extraordinary aptitude for concealment. When Ajay decided to test him, Joginder, with a few pointers from Sharmaji, rendered such a convincing portrayal of a crooked cop taking a bribe that he was immediately inducted into their team.

But though Joginder was now making more money through his association with them than he had ever made in his life, he still lived in the same place, a couple of kilometres from the New Delhi railway station, in a tiny flat that housed his wife and all the homeless cousins who came to them for help and shelter. Some things are hard to change, especially if they make up who you are.

After hanging up on Joginder, Ajay looked around, picked up a pencil and a notepad, and sat down to dial a number. It was answered on the first ring. Clearly, Sharmaji had been waiting beside the telephone. Ajay could hear the shahnai in the background in an internecine auditory conflict with the cackle of voices, the determined efforts of antakshari, and all the other sounds of a Hindu wedding.

'Ajay? Anything in the news?'

'No. We're safe. How's the wedding going?'

Sharmaji sighed. 'I'm going mad, Ajay! I don't think it was this crazy even at my own wedding. There's always something going wrong—'

Ajay interrupted. 'It's normal, Sharmaji. The father of the bride is always the most harried man at a wedding. You're no different. And anyway, what about your first daughter's wedding? How was that different?'

'Ajay, I hadn't met you then! There was no way I could arrange a lavish wedding even if I wanted to!'

'I know, Sharmaji, I know,' said Ajay soothingly.

'I'm alone here. When the hell are you guys coming?'

'Friday. Anything you need from Bombay?'

'Nothing, nothing, Ajay. I just need you guys to get here,' said Sharmaji. 'Although, listen, I just thought of something. Can you just get me a few cartons of those imported cigarettes? For the in-laws, you know…' His voice trailed off.

Ajay smiled, his pen already scratching words on the pad.

'Sure. Anything else?'

'Oh, nothing, nothing. Just remembered it. It's not like I have a list, you know,' said Sharmaji. Ajay imagined his hand digging into the pocket of his sherwani, and emerging with a chit of paper.

'Of course not, of course not. Erm, so is there anything else you… remember?'

'Well, off the top of my head…' There was a pause. 'You know, I couldn't find a good watch for the groom…'

'I'll find one. And...?' Ajay was scribbling away now.

'Maybe a VCR, and a toaster. Get the Philips one, that seems to be the best. And god alone knows what a juicer grinder is, because I have no idea. Perhaps a pair of shoes from Bata too? Size nine, without laces, that seems to be the fashion nowadays... How about a perfume or something too?' He paused for breath.

'I'll get one. A car?'

'No, thanks, I've booked one here. Let me know when you're arriving, Ajay, I'll send someone to pick you up. I guess you might have some luggage?'

Ajay looked at the list. 'Yes, there'll be some luggage. You should really make a list one of these days, Sharmaji. Remembering all these things...'

'I really should, shouldn't I?' said Sharmaji.

'See you on Friday,' said Ajay, and hung up, smiling. It was a regular charade they enacted, and try as he might, he couldn't ever get Sharmaji to make a direct request.

The last call he made was to the henpecked Iqbal in Jaipur. As it turned out, he was being pecked at even as the call went through.

Ajay thought of the one time he had seen Malti, Iqbal's wife. Formidable, that was the only word he could find to describe her, and it fit her perfectly. Iqbal brought in the dough, but there was no doubt who wore the pants in the family, even if said pants were long oversized nightgowns that would've seemed breezy to the average sumo wrestler.

It was Iqbal's son who picked up the phone, and between the time he fetched his father, Ajay heard the stentorian voice deliver various renditions of Wash The Clothes, Hire A Maid Because Don't You Know I Can't Work All Day, and Where's The Tea, You Lazy Lie-Abed. By the time Iqbal came on the line, Ajay was already feeling sorry for him.

'Sorry man, a little work, you know...' Iqbal's voice petered out. There really was no way to alleviate the situation.

'I understand. Malti at home?'

'No, no!' said Iqbal, a tad too quickly. 'She's at the doctor's.'

'Iqbal, are you washing clothes?'

'What? Clo – oh no, not clothes! Just my handkerchief, you know, got a little dirty. Thought I'd get it in the water and—*what are you doing here*?'

The last was directed at his wife, Ajay realized. He heard her say, 'Where's the tea?'

Iqbal must have thought he'd covered the mouthpiece properly, but Ajay could hear the muffled voices quite clearly. 'Stop it! It's the head office! This is important, woman!'

'So?' Malti went on, unfazed. 'Tell them to send us a maid. I can't do everything myself!' With that parting shot, she stampeded away.

'Hello, Ajay?'

'I'm here.'

'Anything in the papers?' said Iqbal, anxious to navigate to a safer conversation.

'Nothing. Looks clear.'

'Good, good. Okay then!'

Ajay couldn't resist. 'So when are you making us tea?'

'Hey, man, come on!'

Ajay burst out laughing. 'Iqbal, that's one fairy tale you have there!'

'Yeah, yeah. Laugh away, wise guy. We'll see how you like it when you're married.'

'Sure,' said Ajay, holding back his mirth. 'Pack up soon. See you at the wedding.'

'See you. And Ajay?' Iqbal's voice held a note of pleading now. 'Don't tell the others, please. They'll rag me to death! You know what they're like...'

'Don't worry,' said Ajay, chuckling. 'They won't hear it from me.'

'Thanks. Bye.'

'Bye,' said Ajay, and hung up.

He looked at the list Sharmaji had given him. He'd already told Joginder to get rid of everything except a few items that he'd thought the older man might need. As it turned out, his guess had been absolutely right.

9

Chase in Chandigarh

The phone on my desk rang. It was Hakim, one of my oldest informers.

'Sir, I've got some news on that fellow.'

I nodded in the universal way everyone does on the phone, even though they know the person at the other end can't see it.

'Good. What news?'

'He's getting his daughter married.'

'Which daughter?'

'Fourth, sir.'

'When?'

'In a few hours.'

'This evening? Couldn't you have told me this earlier, you idiot?'

The man managed to sound wounded, even over the phone. 'Sir, you wanted information, didn't you? I got you that. I didn't know when—'

'All right, all right. Where?'

'His house.'

'Good. And the guests?'

'I kept watch, sir. Didn't see anything strange.'

'Okay. Keep your eyes peeled for anything else.'

I hung up and turned to Rahul and Ranveer who were listening. 'We need to move quickly. Sharma is getting his fourth daughter married tonight. We have to get there as soon as possible.'

Rahul jumped up. 'I'm on it, sir,' he said, and ran out.

Luck seemed to be smiling upon us. A rare occurrence, and something I didn't entirely trust.

'Ranveer, what was the name of the woman who was with you on the raid?'

'Shanti, sir.'

'Yes. Get in touch with Shanti. Tell her to wire as many details about the four men as she can to us. Women notice things that sometimes men don't, they see things differently. Maybe she'll be able to tell us if any of the others are also disgruntled ex-cops.'

'Okay, sir.'

Rahul was back. 'No train tickets, sir. All—'

I broke in. 'No, Rahul, forget the train. We'll take a flight. It's his daughter's wedding. Which means he'll have invited the whole gang. They'll all be there, till tomorrow at least. Find out if there's a flight we can take today.'

'Yes, sir.'

My earlier distrust of luck was soon vindicated; within minutes. Rahul returned, disappointed. 'Sir, there are no flights till tomorrow afternoon.'

'Damn! Are you sure?'

'Yes, sir. I doublechecked,' said Rahul a tad reproachfully.

'Hmm, all right, if there are no flights today evening, we'll drive to Chandigarh. It won't take us more than six to eight hours. By morning, we should be at the wedding venue.'

'What's the rush, sir?' Ranveer asked. He seemed genuinely puzzled. 'It's his daughter's wedding, and if he's invited the other gang members, they'll surely stay for the next couple of days?'

It's good to ask questions. But pointless to ask the wrong ones. I guess the kid would learn in time.

'Ranveer, I still believe that Sharma is not the brains behind the gang. There's someone else who's pulling the strings. And *that* guy is clever. Enough to know that sooner or later, the police will be on his tail. He'd be reckless to go to the wedding at all, but he'd be a moron to stay there for longer than a day. And a moron he is not, you can take it from me.'

I left him to mull over my little impromptu speech and went out into the street, to the shack behind HQ. Looking around to make sure nobody was around, I gave vent to my only vice, and lit up. Ah, it felt good!

Often, my inspiration came from one of these solitary smoking sessions. I'd cracked many a case, after a silent, reflective smoke in this dull, sunless alley. Before quitting.

The nicotine-tinged smoke filled me with a sense of calm that I desperately needed. If things went well, we would have the entire gang under arrest by tomorrow evening. But events seldom play out the way you want them to. And it seemed too easy. A gang that had eluded the police of several states for over three years would most certainly not allow itself to be caught at a wedding.

But my happy, nicotine-filled brain told me, they all make mistakes. Given enough time, everyone screws up. You just have to be patient.

The smoke wasn't helping very much this time. Five minutes later, I went back inside, no more enlightened and only a little calmer than when I'd stepped out.

I gave instructions to every informer in the area who was watching the wedding to keep reporting back to us every half hour. That way, we would miss nothing and also get news of any unusual incident almost immediately. After all, it would be several hours before we arrived at Sharma's house, and the birds might very easily have flown by then. I just hoped they wouldn't.

I summoned Rahul to my office. 'Call the local police. Tell them that there's going to be a heist soon. They should be ready.'

The efficient Rahul was on it instantly. A minute later, he handed me the phone.

'Yes? Sector 17 police station,' a voice drawled over the line. 'What do you want?'

'This is Waseem Khan, CBI Deputy Commissioner of Police. Who the hell is in charge?'

There was a squawk, and I could tell the man was taking a moment to readjust his standard usage voice and vocabulary. A moment later, he spoke again, his tone the perfect combination of respect and sycophancy. 'Sir, I am the duty officer, sir,' he gasped.

'Listen to me very carefully, my man,' I snapped. 'There will be a robbery soon. Somewhere. Some men will pose as the CBI or the police or whatever, I don't know, and raid some place. I don't know where, but it's going to happen, unless you keep your eyes and ears open. Get everyone ready.'

'Now? But—but it's just five thirty in the morning, sir!'

'What makes you think I care?'

There was a pause, and a further readjustment. 'Umm. I'll call the inspector—'

'I don't give a fuck who you have to call. Get on your feet, get your butt moving, and get your people ready. We'll be there this evening, so you'd better have some results. Got it?'

'Yes SIR!' Pause. '*You're* coming? The CBI is coming?'

'Yes. This evening,' I said and hung up. I knew there'd been no need to be rude, but the harsh truth is that it gets the job done. I could always make it up later. Or maybe not.

Rahul looked at me quizzically. 'Will that do any good, sir?'

I sighed. 'Not really. But at least now they know what's coming.'

Rahul just nodded sympathetically, probably accustomed to my gruff ways by now.

He also briefed me about his call to Shanti. Concise, precise, entirely devoid of anything of any use. There went another potential lead. If only more intelligent people were recruited by the police force in our country, there would be fewer crimes.

Or so I told myself.

Those hours were some of the most restless I've ever spent. We kept getting calls with updates, but nothing seemed to be out of the ordinary. Except for the fact that the wedding was a lavish affair, which was strange for a man who didn't even appear to have an official job. Clearly, we had hit pay dirt.

Finally, we left the office and were on our way to Chandigarh. The bad roads and lack of light on the highways slowed us down. We took over nine hours to get to our destination. By the time we entered the city, I had activated my informer network.

We had a small scare by the time of the third call. One of my informers called to say that four men had left the house early in the morning in a taxi, at a time when everyone else in the house was asleep. Sharmaji was one of those who left, but the informer didn't know who the others were. All he could tell us was that the three had arrived the previous afternoon, laden with gifts, and seemed quite ordinary.

It was them. I knew it, I felt it in my bones. It had to be them. Why else would you sneak out of a wedding party the next morning? And where could they be heading?

I'd been on many high-profile cases with Rahul in tow. We'd made many last-minute dashes on planes from one part of the country to another. Once, we'd even flown from Delhi to Amsterdam, hot on the heels of an underworld gangster.

This was the first high-profile case that had required us to undertake such an ignominious journey: along bumpy national highways. Finally, we arrived at the Sector 17 police station, where my message had clearly been passed around, judging from the crowd of cops there to greet us.

'Yes, yes, glad to meet you,' I grumbled as the hundredth cop – or so it seemed – came to shake hands. I grabbed Rahul and said, 'Find me that inspector, now.'

Within the next minute, the three of us were inside the cabin of Station House Officer Param Bir Singh.

'I'm sorry, sir,' he said. 'I got your message, and I've personally been checking the entire area. Nobody's reported any robberies.'

'Then you should make sure you don't post deaf morons as your duty officers,' I said. I'd meant it to rankle, but it didn't seem to have any effect.

'I don't understand,' said Singh, his honest face screwed up in genuine incomprehension.

'I told your man that some men would be posing as cops and raiding some place. I did *not* say robbery, so I fail to see what gave him that impression.'

The scathing tone didn't have any effect. Singh scratched his head. 'I see. Well, I've told everyone to keep track of everything that happens today, but so far, it's just the usual, sir. Chain snatching, a few brawls, nothing more.'

That didn't sound right. 'Have you kept a watch on the house? Sharma's house?'

Singh nodded. 'Yes, sir, we did. Nothing happening there either, sir. Just the usual.'

It certainly didn't sound right. Was I wrong then? I was certain that they would have been up to something, but—

The phone rang. Singh picked it up, listened for a second, and turned to me. 'It's for you, sir.'

'Yeah?'

It was Mohan. 'Sir, one of your informers called. Those four men just returned to the house in a taxi.'

'When?'

'They've just arrived, sir.'

'Good, thanks.'

'Sir, they're unloading some packets from the taxi.'

'All right, I got it.'

I slammed the phone down. 'They're back. Come on. We've got to get to Sharma's house. Singh, get us there as fast as you can!' I shouted, heading out of the room and towards the exit.

All credit to Singh. Rallying from his earlier slowness, he rose to the occasion magnificently. In less than a minute, he had a couple of jeeps ready, and we were racing through the narrow streets, high-pitched sirens blaring at full volume. Singh was with Ranveer and me in our car, Rahul and a few other local policemen in the other. I filled the Chandigarh man in on the way, as succinctly as I could.

'They're doing it under our nose, Singh. This sort of thing can't be encouraged,' I yelled over the din. 'We have to make sure everyone knows who's the boss.'

'I agree,' he screeched back. 'Will you arrest them?'

I smiled grimly. 'That's the plan.'

Plans, though, have a nasty habit of falling apart at the last minute.

With a veritable maniac behind the wheel, we reached the house in record time, covering nearly ten kilometres in fifteen minutes. Tyres screeched as the two jeeps shuddered to a halt, and Rahul, Ranveer and Singh were out in a flash, drawing their guns as they barged through the gate. I followed at a slower pace.

A strange sight greeted my eyes as I walked through the gate. Rahul, Singh and a few other cops were yelling at the top of their voices, guns in hand, pointing at four men who were lying stretched out on the floor. Ranveer was standing a little further off, looking at the prostrate figures with a strange expression. The two-storey house was ablaze with light. People hung out of every single window, watching the drama unfold with the knowledge that there was a safe distance between them and what was happening.

An imposing woman of matronly proportions was standing at the main door, a rolling pin in hand, arguing ferociously with a constable who appeared to be trying to pacify her.

As I approached the four figures on the

ground, the early-morning light was enough to tell me that we had been fooled. Even from behind, I could easily tell that neither of the four men was Sharma. I turned towards Ranveer and caught his eye, and almost imperceptibly, he shook his head, holstering his weapon.

Time to take charge.

I strode forward, past the array of hand-held weaponry, and knelt beside the figures. 'You, in the centre. Who are you?'

'Sir, I'm nobody. I've not done anything wrong. This is a mistake—'

I cut in. 'I'll decide that. Now shut up and just tell me who you are and what you're doing here.'

The man whimpered. 'Sir, please believe me, we are nobody. A man came to us and gave us some money, told us to deliver some packets to this address. That's all we know.'

'He's lying,' snarled Singh. 'Let's bash in his head, or perhaps a limb he doesn't really need. Maybe that will give him some incentive!'

The man panicked. By now, all four were gibbering with fright. No way could they be the gang we were looking for.

'No, Singh. Let it be. These guys are nothing.'

Singh was about to say something when the wireless set on his belt crackled. Holstering his gun, an act that brought an expression of hopeful relief to the faces of the four unfortunate men, he barked into it, 'Yes?'

'Sir, you told me to keep a watch?'

'Yes, yes, I remember. What is it?'

'Sir, it's not here. It's in Ludhiana. I just had a call from a friend of mine there. He said four men robbed the residence of an actor.'

'WHAT? When?'

'A couple of hours ago, I believe.'

Singh turned towards me, wide-eyed. But there was more to come.

We were looking at another nightmarish road trip, this time to Ludhiana, about 150 km from Sharma's house.

Rahul and I began discussing the odds that our targets were still there.

Perhaps I could just send Rahul and Ranveer to Ludhiana, and return to Delhi.

Then the radio crackled again: 'Sir, just got an alert from Sadar police station about four men who duped a major electronics store in Sadar Bazar in Ludhiana. We got a call at the local police station.'

I grabbed the radio. 'What kind of shop?'

'Imported goods, sir. Illegal. Apparently it was a customs raid.'

'Shit! When was this?'

'About half an hour ago.'

I threw the radio back to Singh. 'You,' I said, pointing to one of the horizontal figures. 'Where did they meet you?'

'Sir, outside Rock Garden.'

'When?'

'Around four a.m.' The man was trembling.

'Did they say why?'

'I don't know, sir,' he cried. 'They just gave us the money, the address and the packets. I don't know anything else, sir, honest.'

I grabbed the man by the collar and pulled him upright. Then, leaning in so close that I could smell the stale beer on his breath, I spoke through gritted teeth, 'Think very carefully. Was there anything else? Because if there's anything you're hiding, I'll have your life in my hands, do you understand? You'll never see your mother or father or brother or sister ever again, because you'll spend the rest of your miserable life inside a ten-by-ten cell.'

The man stared back at me, speechless.

'So. Is. There. Anything. Else.'

'Sir, they s-s-s-said they were g-g-g-going to the Ludhiana s-s-s-station,' he managed to stammer out.

Station? Oh dear god!

'Rahul,' I shouted, flinging the man back down. 'Check those packets. What's in them?'

Rahul snatched up one, and slit it open. It was filled with paper. He snatched up another; that one was stuffed with toys, the ones you get on every roadside.

He looked up at me in dismay.

They'd done it again. Somehow, they knew that we'd be coming, they'd known that the wedding would be watched. And so they'd planned ahead.

But it wasn't too late.

I turned to Singh. 'How far is Ludhiana junction from here?'

'Sir, two hours, tops.'

'Do you have any idea when any main line express leaves the station?' I was getting desperate.

'Sir, I have in-laws in Ludhiana. I know that the first express train leaves the station for Delhi at ten forty a.m.'

I looked at my watch. It was just 9 a.m. They'd left for the station at 8.30. Maybe, just maybe, we could catch them at the station.

I pointed to one of the others lying prostrate on the ground. 'You! Did they say where they were going?' I asked, knowing it was a long shot.

He shook his head. So much for that.

'Singh, get some of your men to interrogate these fellows. See what else they know. But don't be too hopeful. I want you to question the people in the house too.'

'Yes, sir.'

'And get someone to check all trains that leave between nine and eleven, even if they are metre-gauge trains. And I need your driver. The maniac, the one who drove us here.'

Singh looked puzzled. 'Why him, sir?'

'How long did you say it would take to reach the station?'

'Two hours.'

'We need to get there in one. I need him.'

10

Wedding Windfall

Ajay could not help marvelling at how, no matter how many daughters he married off, Sharmaji always managed to be as flustered, as harrowed and as clueless as he'd been at his own wedding. He'd been to the second daughter's wedding, then the third, and now the fourth, and every time, Sharmaji seemed completely out of his depth. At least until the rest of the gang came along and provided, quite apart from the material requirements, moral support.

Last night, after everyone had gone to bed – having exhausted themselves – the four of them had sat around drinking and quietly chatting.

'So, Sharmaji,' said Ajay, 'how many daughters do you have left to marry off?'

'L-l-let's shee now,' muttered the tipsy father of the bride, considering the question with utmost seriousness. 'There's Mrs Sharma—'

'What, you want to marry her off?' said Joginder innocently, as the others started laughing. 'What did she do?'

'Do? Oh, you shaid daughtersh! I have eight daughtersh. You hear that? Eight!'

'Parminder,' said Ajay.

'Harvinder,' said Iqbal.

'Garvinder,' said Joginder.

'Yesh yesh! Then there's Satvinder, Mohinder, Surinder, Maninder and—and—Sukhwinder, my youngesht,' he ended happily, and drained his glass.

There was a silence. Each of the other three was contemplating asking the question they'd had in their heads since they'd discovered the nursery rhyme-like nomenclature in the Sharma household. But they hadn't wanted to offend Sharmaji, and so had refrained.

Iqbal took a deep breath, and took the leap at last, witnessing the man's drunkenness. 'Sharmaji, you've got some wonderfully named children,' he said.

Sharmaji looked at them. They looked back. He cleared his throat. 'I know,' he said. 'They kept coming, and we were fine till the first three, and they still kept coming, and there were so many names to think of, and—and—and we didn't have any TV back in our day!' he finished wretchedly.

The three looked at each other, close to laughter. Best leave it at that, they thought.

But Sharmaji wasn't done. He gazed at his glass, whose contents had emptied like the happiness had drained from his face a minute ago. 'Y' know, boys, a wedding's a shad shad thing. My girlsh will all go away! I will be left all alone—'

Ajay winked at him. 'So what, Sharmaji! Get some more Harvinders and Sukhwinders and Maninders!'

Sharmaji seemed most offended. 'You—you—Ajay, all thish ish a joke to you! Jusht you wait till you marry and have a girl. You'll know what—my poor girlsh!' he lapsed back into silence.

The words seemed to sober Ajay; he immediately went quiet. Before the others could notice and comment, though, Sharmaji went on, 'Yeah, and it'sh coshtly too! So many kidsh—I'm broke now, and I've got more kidsh to get married! Hey-ho!' He looked at his glass and decided another swig would make him feel less morose.

Ajay looked up. 'All right, Sharmaji, stop crying and tell me something. Have you heard of Satwar Singh?'

Sharmaji paused, mid-gulp, and thought hard. 'The Punjabi actor?'

Ajay nodded.

Iqbal spoke. 'I've seen the fellow. He came to Jaipur last month. Some big shop near our house was being inaugurated, and they'd brought him.'

'So what do you think of him?' Ajay asked Iqbal.

'Oh, he's the usual rich bastard. Came in some swanky car, looked like he owned the place. I heard he'd even asked the shopowners to pay for his makeup!'

'Black money, Iqbal bhai, it's all black money,' said Ajay.

They looked at him, surprised. 'How do you know that?' demanded Sharmaji.

Ajay smiled his enigmatic smile. 'Have another drink, Sharmaji,' he said, pouring one liberally for the older man.

'Have you ever seen an actor begging for mercy in real life?' asked Ajay.

'I would definitely want to see one some day,' Joginder chimed in.

Ajay got to his feet. 'Let's make a spectacle of the actor. It's four a.m. now, if we leave now we'll reach Ludhiana by six.'

Sharmaji – who was already drifting away to the few hours of sleep he would need to fully recover from the drinking – opened his eyes blearily when Ajay shook him from his semi-conscious state. He was about to yell at him when he saw the expression on Ajay's face.

The man's eyes were sparkling, which meant they were going to make a killing.

Sharmaji was wide awake in an instant. Ten minutes later, he was ready. Avoiding all the men in their various stages of sleep, he left the house through the back entrance and walked briskly to the end of the lane. There he met the others, who had gone ahead and were waiting for him in a taxi.

The four of them sat mute in the car, unrecognizable in their disguises.

Something was not right. Ajay felt it instinctively. His gut feeling had never failed him yet. And right now, as their car drove towards Ludhiana and raced down the highway from Sharmaji's house, his intuition was screaming at him to stop.

'Joginder, pull over here.'

Surprised, Joginder did as he was told. He pulled up near the pavement. Chandigarh's famous Rock Garden lay just ahead.

'What's wrong, Ajay?' asked Sharmaji, concerned.

Ajay didn't reply; he just sat there, his eyes unfocused, his mind clearly far away. In the rear-view mirror, Sharmaji and Iqbal, both in the back seat, saw Ajay's eyes locked on a point ahead of them in ferocious concentration.

Just as abruptly as they had come to a halt, Ajay snapped out of his thoughts. 'Change of plans. I'm sorry, Sharmaji, but you won't be happy with what I'm going to say.'

Sharmaji sighed resignedly. 'Out with it.'

'We can't go back.'

There was a collective gasp. 'What do you mean, we can't go back? Go back where?' cried Iqbal.

'We can't go back to my house,' said Sharmaji. 'Isn't that what you're saying, Ajay?'

Ajay nodded. 'I'm afraid so. There's a good chance that by the time we return, the police will be waiting for us at your house. We can't take that risk.'

The three of them watched Sharmaji struggle with the idea. He would be leaving his family on the day after the wedding, when his daughter had just gone away to her new house, her new family. His wife, for one, would be livid. His family that had come from afar would certainly complain too.

On the other hand, going back meant never getting to see any of them again. And in all the seven years he had worked with Ajay, the boy had not been wrong even once.

He sighed again. 'Bugger it. At least let me call my wife.'

Ajay nodded. Sharmaji got off and lumbered over to a nearby phone booth.

'So, what do we do now, Ajay?' said Joginder.

Ajay looked around. Something caught his attention. Without turning his head, he rolled down his window and pointed across the road. 'See those four men? They're our ticket out of here.'

The taxi dropped them off at a mechanic's place, where a fat wad of money got them a white government Ambassador for the day. For what they were planning, it would certainly have to be *this* car. Soon, they were on the road to Ludhiana, with Joginder at the wheel. He didn't stop at a single traffic signal, the flashing red beacon on top of the car acting as an instant green light. All the people at a roadside dhaba where they broke journey, including its owner, would have sworn to the fact that four men from the CBI had walked in, flashed their IDs, asked for food, wolfed down a scrumptious breakfast and left. All of them would also vouch that their leader, a fattish man with a deep voice and a bushy moustache, made sure he paid before they left.

Naturally, none of them could vouch for the fact that the man hadn't had a moustache the previous night.

By 6 a.m., they had arrived at their destination, which was being guarded by a couple of burly guards. They looked very surprised when a government vehicle stopped in front of them, and the windows rolled down to reveal four very official-looking men sitting inside. But they stood their ground, safe in the knowledge that their employer had paid the right kinds of people.

The first guard walked up to the car and spoke, affecting boredom. 'Yes, what do you want?'

'We want to meet your hero, chum,' said Sharmaji.

You had to hand it to the fellow, he had balls. 'Fuck off,' he said. 'He's shooting.'

But it was hard to browbeat Sharmaji when he was in full form. His eyes not leaving the guard's, he opened the door and got out, treating him to a full view of his massive frame. 'Really?' he said, walking right up to the man until they were face to face. Well, face to chest. 'Which film?'

The guard made a strangled noise in his throat. 'Um... *Jawani ka Jalwa,*' he hazarded.

In a flash, Sharmaji had swatted him aside with one massive paw. As the man lay on the ground, rubbing his bruised cheek, he strode to the other guard, who by this time had decided that cooperation was the best option. But before he could get this realization across, Sharmaji had hauled him up by the arms and shoved an ID that said 'CBI' in his face.

A minute later, the four of them were inside the bungalow, flashing IDs left, right and centre at curious servants. A tray-laden chef was subject to a P.K. Sharma slap, which instantly bought obedience from everyone else. As Sharmaji stamped about, the others played out their roles, which they had rehearsed and performed umpteen times, to perfection.

Iqbal headed straight for the bar in the lounge, ripped it open, and began stuffing expensive imported alcohol bottles in a bag.

Joginder eyed a huge painting for a few seconds. Then he went over and slid it to one side, revealing the predictable hidden safe. He signalled to Sharmaji; the 'leader' started shouting and elicited a response from the head chef, who, prompted by both his previous experience of the slap and the possibility of more in the future, immediately gave up the combination.

Ajay bounded up the rounded stairs to the biggest door he could find, kicked it open, and saw exactly what he had expected to see.

The room was mammoth, easily half the size of his flat in Bombay. In the centre was a bed, which now disgorged a nude woman who ran screaming, all parts of her body bouncing interestingly, to the bathroom. Remaining in the bed was the actor Satwar Singh, who had clearly been awoken by said screaming.

'Wha—' he started sleepily. Then he saw Ajay, who said brightly, 'Good morning!'

That woke him up. Covering his flab with a dressing gown, the thespian clambered off the bed. 'Who the hell are you?' he shrieked.

'Fans, Mr Singh,' said Ajay, winking at him. 'We really wanted to meet you, so we thought we'd drop in!'

For a second, the answer floored the actor. Then he found his voice and lost his temper. 'Who the fuck do you think you are? Get out! Get the hell out. I'll skin you alive—'

His threats were cut short; Ajay took a leaf out of Sharmaji's book and let fly a ringing slap, bringing Singh to his knees. Then he took out his ID card and knelt down himself. 'Look at this. This is who I am. I know all about you, you piece of shit. I know you're a bloody drug dealer, and you like kissing the arse of the underworld.'

By the time Ajay had half pushed, half pulled the protesting actor out of the room and downstairs, Joginder had already prised open shelves in the kitchen and discovered the predictable packets of drugs.

There wasn't much Singh could say now. He was trembling. He could hear the disconcertingly hushed voices of his servants from behind the door to the study, where they'd been cloistered. It was the last blow. 'Sir, please let me go,' he said, pleading, hands folded. 'I'm nobody, I just provide entertainment to people, I only—'

There was a shout from outside. 'Sir, you've got to see this!' shouted Iqbal excitedly. Ajay, his face black as thunder, looked at Singh, who seemed to have frozen.

The three of them went outside, Ajay dragging the actor along.

Iqbal was standing next to a massive, rapidly emptying swimming pool. They watched with incredulity as the last of the water drained away to reveal the door of a safe set into the wall of the pool.

Finally, the actor broke. Without any protest, he allowed himself to be led down the stairs and unlocked the door. The gang was completely unprepared for what they saw.

The two-foot-large secret crevice was filled with gold and silver biscuits, lining the wall right up to the ceiling. It was the biggest safe they'd seen and, but for a chance reflection off the water that Iqbal had been lucky enough to catch, they would have missed it altogether.

Feigning patience, the gang of four carried out the rest of their 'chores'. Everything was packed up in two gunny bags. The actor, now crying bitterly, was made to sign on an official-looking paper. He was then taken to his bedroom and locked in. Iqbal disconnected the phone lines. Finally, fifteen minutes later, they were on their way, richer by several lakhs and hardly believing their luck. The 'raid' had taken less than an hour in all.

But Ajay seemed dissatisfied. The others didn't notice it, so mesmerized were they with their latest catch. The drugs had disturbed him; he was getting sidelined from his path, his endgame. The drugs they'd found had brought it home to him.

Before they caught on to his mood, he

overrode his thoughts. At least now, he would celebrate. In fact…

'Sharmaji, weren't you saying you wanted to give more electronic goods to your daughter for her wedding?' he said, his eyes on the road. He'd chosen to drive while the others counted the loot.

'I was, I really was, Ajay!' said Sharmaji. 'I'd promised myself that if I could afford to, I would give her more dowry. I can't believe you remember!'

Iqbal, who was looking out of the car, now said, 'Hey, this isn't the road back home. This is the way to Sadar Bazar.'

'Yes, it is. I thought since we organized gold and cash earlier, we would organize some imported electronic items too, for the wedding,' said Ajay, smiling.

Sharmaji beamed at him. 'You're a good man.'

They spent the rest of the journey in a carefree mood, as if they'd just learnt they had scored big in an exam and owed it to themselves to have fun. As they entered the Sadar Bazar area, the electronics market was yet to open but breakfast and mithai shops were doing brisk business. The foursome stopped for breakfast at an expensive restaurant and then some jalebis at a roadside stall.

The jalebis made Sharmaji nostalgic. 'You know, boys,' he said, munching away on one, eyes half-closed in satisfaction, 'your Mrs Sharma and I used to do this exact same thing. After college, we would spend hours just roaming the streets, chatting and laughing.' He paused to slurp the jalebi juice off his wrist, and resumed, 'She would always want something. I had to buy her stuff all the time, but my father would never give me enough money, so everything I bought her was cheap.'

Iqbal joined in. 'You're right, Sharmaji. Maybe I should take back something for Malti and Rahul too.'

'Sure, why don't we—' Joginder started to say, and stopped.

Ajay's thoughts went to Priya and her warm embrace. He excused himself and went in search of an STD booth.

'How are you doing, Cleopatra?'

'What an opening. You seem to be in a good mood.

'I actually tried calling you last night, but each time Shakaal answered.'

'Why Shakaal?'

'Arre, your father and the villain of *Shaan* both have shiny pates.' Ajay smiled mischievously, though his beloved couldn't see him.

'Achcha, tell me when you are coming to Bombay?' Priya asked.

'Will come soon, and this time it will be to take you away for good,' Ajay replied.

He returned to his friends in a much better mood. 'Guys, if you are done with jalebis and lassi, it's time to decorate our houses.'

The four of them looked around carefully. They hadn't chosen the best place for a shopping expedition. They were in a street that reeked of high society, with shops that catered exclusively to the rich and the neo-rich. All imported goods stores, boasting products from all over the world. Gadgets, clothes, goods, even some exotic foods – everything the rich liked to spend money on. Most certainly not a place for men like them, even if they did have more than anyone could imagine in the trunk of their car.

Ajay winked at the others, and together they went into the nearest restaurant. In a few minutes, they came back out, but they certainly weren't the same men who had gone in. The loo inside the restaurant had come in handy. The moustached, frowning Sharmaji strode towards a store, followed by the stick-thin, slightly cross-eyed Joginder, who sported sunglasses and a false beard. Iqbal was a full-bearded turbaned Sikh and Ajay was – well, himself. He had never needed too much of disguise; early on in life he'd realized that he had one of those faces which you might see every day, yet never quite register. A thoroughly nondescript, forgettable face.

They were all dressed in immaculate formal clothes, and looked menacingly official. Sharmaji was confidently striding towards the nearest shop when Ajay grabbed his arm. 'No,' he said. 'Not that one.' He pointed to one at the corner. 'There. More cover.'

The others knew better than to ask why. Ajay was phenomenally accurate at spotting the right place to raid. They just hadn't gotten around to asking how he did it.

Ajay led the way. There was no plan, the others just followed him.

The men barged in through the door of their target shop as if they owned the place, pushing various knickknacks out of the way. Before anyone in the shop could react, Ajay said, 'Down the shutters now. Take this place apart. You—' He pointed to a couple of customers. 'Get out, now. This is a raid.'

The shop emptied in less than thirty seconds. Iqbal drew the shutters down from inside, turned around and folded his hands across his chest, in a gesture that smacked of finality.

The owner hurried forward, a tiny man in his forties who looked as if he'd just bathed in oil.

'Who are you?' and 'What the hell is going on here?' were the two conventional openings. It was always those two. Ajay waited.

'What's the meaning of this?'

Ah. Sometimes people don't believe in following convention.

'Customs,' snapped Ajay.

'Customs?' repeated the man. 'But I've paid the duty fees!'

Ajay grabbed the man by the collar and dragged him to the counter. 'Show me your receipts.' He pointed to a man in his twenties who looked like an offspring of Frankenstein's monster and a banshee. 'You, take sir…' He indicated Sharmaji. '…and show him around the shop. Don't hide anything, you hear?'

Turning back to the owner, Ajay saw that he was holding out a stack of papers. He'd got them too quickly, and he looked a little too composed. Ajay selected a receipt at random, took one glance at it, and without warning, slapped the man hard.

'What the fuck is this? You trying to screw with me, shithead? Where's your import licence?'

The shock on the man's face was enough proof for Ajay, he'd broken Mr Oily.

'Running a smuggling racket, are you, you little weasel?' Ajay shouted.

The man fell down, groping at Ajay's feet. 'Please, sir, your honour, sir, I'm a poor man, please—'

'You? Poor? What the fuck do you think I am, stupid? How many people have paid with their lives for a little piece of shit like you?'

The man pleaded. 'Your honour, sir, let me go. Please, sir, your highness, take what you want, please let me go. I won't smuggle anymore…'

Not many people noticed when, a few minutes later, four men lifted the shutters of a shop and walked out with sixteen bags bearing the store's logo. And not many noticed that the store didn't do any business that day.

Not until they were in the car and on their way back home did the others burst into laughter. Ajay joined in too, smiling.

'Ajay, how the hell did you know which shop would be...?' Sharmaji said.

Ajay shrugged. 'No idea. I guess I just knew.'

'Did you know they were smugglers?' said Iqbal, still feeling a little awed.

'I think so. I mean, I didn't know for sure,' said Ajay. 'But you know what, Iqbal? I was born with a nose for it. It's a scent that leads me to these kinds of men.'

There was a pause. Then Sharmaji said, 'What, like a dog?'

They all burst out laughing again.

11

A Close Shave

Sharmaji wiped the sweat off his forehead. 'Jogi, go get us tea, there's a good fellow!'

Grumbling, Joginder got off the train and went in search of a vendor.

They were on the Paschim Express, the train which originates at Amritsar and terminates at Bombay Central station, halting at Ludhiana junction for ten minutes along the way. It was 10.30 a.m. They were all in the same coach, but only for a while.

Ask any sane man to get train tickets only an hour before the train departs on an overnight journey and he would swear it was impossible – but Ajay had done the impossible again. As they approached the station, he suddenly told the taxi driver to let him off. 'You guys go on ahead and wait for me near the platform. I'll be right back.'

'But where are we going?' shouted Iqbal as the taxi started to move away.

'Bombay!' Ajay shouted back, before getting lost in the crowd.

They'd hardly been waiting two minutes, all six pairs of eyes glued to their suitcases in careful nonchalance, when Ajay came running up, two envelopes in his hand. 'All right, come on. I've got tickets to Bombay.'

'How the hell did you get them at this time?' said Joginder, amazed. 'The train is expected in… what…'

'In twenty minutes,' finished Ajay.

In a few minutes, the train was heading towards Ludhiana junction. 'I couldn't get seats in the same coach, so we'll be spread out a little,' Ajay said. 'But until the train starts, I want all of us to be in the same coach.'

And there they were, crowding inside the compartment. Their suitcases were in the aisle, and blocked the way neatly for nearly everyone else. Sharmaji had to apologize several times.

Joginder was still grumbling as he balanced the tea cups in his hands and gingerly walked back to the train. But then he saw something that made him forget his irritation.

There were large numbers of people milling about in the station. Among them were the usual suspects: beggars, vendors, ticket checkers, policemen. But suddenly he saw something, just for a fleeting moment, that gave him pause. Maybe everything wasn't as it seemed to be.

A man with a suitcase had just come in through the entrance. Everything about him was fine, except that he seemed to be paying a lot of attention to his surroundings. Too much attention. He looked up at the foot overbridge. At another man who was standing there. The second man gave an imperceptible shake of the head.

It was tiny, but it was enough. The net was closing in. He had to get out of here, and do so without drawing attention. Which was easier said than done with four tea cups in his hands.

Walking past a garbage bin, he surreptitiously dropped one in, and hoped like hell nobody had noticed. Then he drained the second cup in that hand in one gulp. It was scalding, and burned his tongue and throat, and he could feel blisters right down to his gut. He fought back an urge to dance around in pain, but at least that was another cup gone. There.

His luck would've held, had the man who'd just walked in been anyone else. But it was Waseem, and he'd just seen a man drain a scalding cup of tea in one gulp.

Out of the corner of his eye, Joginder saw the man begin to walk a little faster. Trouble was, he was walking *towards* him.

He turned the corner, and knowing he had just a few seconds before the cop rounded the corner too, flung the tea cups away and made a dash for the train.

Ajay was looking out of the window and saw Joginder running. Instantly, he surmised what must have happened. He looked behind Joginder, but didn't see anyone.

Turning quickly to the others, he said, 'All right, what I was afraid of has happened. The cops are here. Yes, Jogi, I know...' – this was to the panting Joginder – 'so all of you, listen to me very carefully.'

I'd spent around two minutes setting up the perimeter, but Singh was a capable man, and I didn't have to spend any more effort on this. I was close to those bastards, I could feel it. They still hadn't left.

All the uniformed guys were outside, and I sent just a few plainclothes men in, through different gates. Too many cops would scare them away.

I walked in, pulling a suitcase I'd just borrowed from a helpful citizen. Well, a citizen who'd been bullied into helpfulness, true, but hey, as long as he got his luggage back, right?

I looked around, spotting familiar faces in the crowd. Nothing seemed out of the ordinary, but then nothing rarely does until it comes up behind you and kicks you where the sun doesn't shine.

I took in as much as I could at a glance. There were a couple of transvestites haranguing a young couple, a group of men sitting in a semicircle playing rummy, a man trying to balance four cups of tea as he walked, a coolie who looked thoroughly bogged down by the weight of the luggage on his head, Ranveer standing on the foot overbridge…

His inexperience showed again. As our eyes met, he shook his head. It was imperceptible, but it shouldn't have been done.

I looked around again, walking slowly ahead, taking care not to bump into anything. And then I saw it. The man with the four cups now had three. Where was the fourth? As I watched, he drained another glass in one mighty gulp. His body stiffened. Jesus, I thought! That tea must have been fucking hot! Why? No man would do that, unless he was forced to.

He was walking faster now, and he was moving away from me. Directly away. That *had* to mean something.

I walked faster too. Out of the corner of my eye, I saw Rahul approach, having seen some purposeful movement from me. Good man.

The fellow made a blind turn. Shit!

I sped to the turning and looked around. The man had disappeared. Damn, damn, damn!

Rahul arrived behind me, but before I could say anything, my walkie-talkie crackled. It was Ranveer. 'Sir, I've got him. The man you were chasing. The man with the tea. He just got into a train.'

'Which one?' I barked.

'I think it's the Paschim Express.'

I turned to Rahul. 'Get outside, find out. This was a last-minute dash, they must have bought the tickets in black. And they must have paid a bomb.'

He nodded and ran off.

Police work is all about following the trail. Every criminal leaves a trail, however intelligent or lowlife he thinks he is. And that's what you have to do as a good cop – follow the trail like a determined bloodhound. There would be enough trips and dead ends on the way, but stay true to the path and in the end, you'll get your man.

Sometimes, though, all you need is sheer, blind luck.

I had no idea why I took my eyes off the train, but I did. And saw a familiar figure walking briskly towards one of the toilets. I'd seen enough pictures of Sharmaji in police files and at his house to recognize him anywhere.

This time, I didn't take my eyes off him. I watched him walk into the men's room. Still not looking anywhere else, I spoke into the radio. 'I've got Sharma. Repeat, I've got

Sharma. Inside men's toilet near platform 4. I want two men here on the double. Repeat, I want two men outside that toilet, and I want them *now*!'

Backup would arrive. In the meantime, it wouldn't do any harm to follow the fellow in.

Slowly, but as naturally as I could, I opened the door to the smelly loo. The fat ass was just in front of me, washing his face.

I walked up behind him, savoured the moment for a second longer than I should have, and said, 'P.K. Sharma, you're mine now.'

In hindsight, I should have sensed something was wrong. Not when the man in front of me didn't swivel around in surprise, not when I suddenly realized that there was not a single urinal in here, not even when I felt the touch of cold steel on my neck. I should have noticed something was not right when I entered a public toilet in broad daylight and found it empty except for just one man. In a crowded station in India, that's just not possible.

But there I was, outwitted, one step too far behind.

The pressure on my neck shifted, and I heard a voice say, 'You will, of course, not move.'

It was the coldest voice I'd ever heard. Enough to induce frostbite in summer. Sheer ruthless menace dripping from it, the voice said, 'Sharmaji, don't turn around. Walk sideways to the door, keep your back to us, and leave.'

Every instruction was followed to the letter.

The man behind me spoke again. 'Your name.' It wasn't a request.

'Waseem Khan.'

'I trust you will not follow me out, Waseem Khan. It won't end well.'

I rallied. 'You have nowhere to go, mister. There are policemen everywhere. Why don't you just give up?'

The man laughed. It was like icicles grating on glass. 'Is that the best line you have? If that represents your intelligence, Waseem Khan, you will never catch me.'

'Listen to me. You can't—'

At that point, I registered a thud; my brain communicated to me that I'd just been hit in the back of the head. It communicated to my legs to fold up beneath me, told my nerves I was hurting like hell, and then I blacked out.

Ajay opened the door to the toilet and walked out. Iqbal was waiting just outside. He reached out as the door closed, and ripped out the 'Gents' sticker. Underneath it, the sign said 'Ladies'.

The two of them walked away slowly, past the two guards who were standing to attention outside the men's toilet, arguing with a couple of men who clearly were having bladder issues. As they passed them, one of the cops' radios crackled and they heard a voice say, 'Sir, Rahul here. Have just got hold of a tout. They're heading to Bombay, sir. Sir?'

There were barely five minutes left for the train's departure. The two of them walked as fast as they could without drawing attention, and got in.

Ajay had regained his composure, but Sharmaji was still looking ashen. 'Ajay, what the hell was that! How did you—'

'No time now, Sharmaji,' Joginder interrupted. 'They know we're going to

Bombay. They know we're on this train. They'll just stop the train at the next station and—'

Ajay interrupted him. 'All of you, go to your seats. First change into your... outfits. Don't worry, we're safe for now.'

With a loud hoot, the train started. The four of them were staring out of the window, looking for any signs of the police. There didn't seem to be any.

Just as the train picked up speed, they saw a man running next to it. He was trying hard to keep up, but was slowly falling behind.

Waseem Khan, thought Ajay. Persistent fellow.

But the train was going too fast now, and Waseem was falling behind. Suddenly, before any of them could stop him, Sharmaji leaned forward, towards the window. Waseem saw him, and his eyes registered the shock; Sharmaji was waving a cheeky goodbye.

The next station, Ambala, was swarming with policemen. They had clearly been told to be on alert, and were checking every passenger thoroughly. They had a detailed description of Sharmaji, and a sketchy one of Joginder.

None of them noticed that among the many people boarding and alighting, four men had got off and met at the ticket counter. The descriptions that the police had didn't match any of them, although if someone pulled at the facial foliage on display, they would have been surprised. One of the men extracted two envelopes from his pocket, one of which had already been torn open. He tore the other one open now, and took out four tickets. He then handed a ticket each to the others.

If anyone had been keeping watch, they would have seen the four men boarding the next train to Howrah, and heading for berths in four different coaches.

12

Looking for Mr X

I made my report to the AD. He wasn't happy. I wasn't either, but then I didn't have to listen to myself shouting at me for having screwed up.

After nearly half an hour's worth of decibel-intensive abuse, I was told to pull up my socks and summarily dismissed. That smarted. Almost more than the humiliation at the station had. I couldn't summon up the courage to ask about the promotion or the increment. Not because I would have been yelled at again, but because they might just block it forever.

I saw the concerned faces of Rahul and Ranveer the moment I returned to our floor.

They were doing their best not to look at me, perhaps fearing they would catch me in a vulnerable moment, and the anxiety radiated off them: tangible, disheartening.

I couldn't think, couldn't process anything. Not just yet. After what had happened yesterday in Chandigarh, I had felt my mind go blank, let my brain shut down. And even now, it had not rebooted properly.

Fuck it all. I needed a smoke.

I went downstairs, out of the building and into the alley. There were a couple of other people there, but only those who had truly got the shit kicked out of them dared go out to this godforsaken place and stand there breathing in its rancid staleness along with the nicotine. We all nodded at each other, not speaking, not needing to. There were no ranks here, only the shared stench of desperation and defeat.

The nicotine switched the power back on in my head. And with it came the shocking realization – I had been beaten. It was the first time that a criminal, a common, petty, low-class breaker of the law had outsmarted me. I, who had spent more than two decades with the best law-enforcement agency in the country, who had put over two hundred crooks, big and small, behind bars. I was the agency's go-to man, the one officer they knew was infallible, who would not go wrong, who they knew would never fail. And I had just failed.

The rage, the hurt, the pride, all that was eating away at me welled up, seeking an outlet, seeking to howl at the world, and in my anger, I aimed a punch at the wall beside me.

Damn fool thing to do. The moment my fist hit the concrete, the pain exploded in my hand, shot up my arm, reverberated right up to my brain. For a full twenty seconds, there was nothing but sheer, mind-numbing pain, and only after that did I come to my senses. I found myself standing clutching my right wrist, which was already bruising. Slowly, through the haze, I looked around and saw, thankfully, that the alley was empty. That was a bit of luck.

And then it hit me. The simplest solution to it all. It was so blindingly obvious, right there in plain sight, and it had taken me another broken promise to myself (the cigarette) and a moronic bit of activity – by which I'd probably broken my wrist – to realize that.

I smiled at nothing in particular, clutched at

my broken wrist again, thanked the nicotine for the epiphany, told myself it wasn't the nicotine, and went back inside.

'What the hell!' cried Ranveer when he saw me. 'What happened to you?'

I grinned at him in manic euphoria. 'It's nothing, just a flesh wound. Listen—'

'Just a flesh wound?' said Rahul, and looked at me oddly. 'Sir, you've broken at least two fingers here!'

'Fingers?' I looked down at my hand. 'I thought it was just the wrist!'

'I said at least.'

I shrugged. 'It was worth it. Forget it. Now listen to me—'

'No, you listen to me,' he interrupted. 'This has to be checked out. You can't go around like this! What if—'

I realized it was time I pulled myself together; I most certainly did not need a 'needs therapy' tag on me, especially now that I was down in the AD's eyes. With a great effort, I gathered myself. It was time to take charge.

'I said, forget it, Rahul.'

He looked at me again, and seemed satisfied this time that his boss was back.

'Listen to me. We've been going about this the wrong way. Remember I told you that Sharma can't be the brains behind the whole thing?'

Rahul and Ranveer nodded.

'Well, now we know I was right. He's not the main man. So who's the main man?' I looked at their faces, and then at the others who were standing gazing at me. They all had the same half-incredulous look.

Then I caught sight of myself in the mirror and sighed. In the reflection, I saw my haggard, stubble-faced, sunken-eyed self, bent over with pain. No wonder they were looking at me so oddly.

No matter. I gestured impatiently. 'All right, all right, you bloody idiots. I'll bloody well get the hand fixed, okay? Now can someone please focus on what I'm saying?'

That seemed to satisfy them. Mohan and Shankar exchanged a knowing glance and went back to their desks. Rahul sat back in the chair, leaving only Ranveer still gazing at my face with a worried expression.

'Wipe that look off your face, man, and grow some balls,' I told Ranveer. 'This is much more important.'

He reddened and assumed an attentive look. Good enough.

'We've been fools,' I told the two of them. 'We've been going at the gang, but we know that when together, they're clearly quite smart. NOT smarter,' I told Rahul, who had just opened his mouth, 'than us, just very, very smart. So we have to make them dumb.'

I waited for the 'How?' to come. It had to be Ranveer.

It was. 'How?'

'We hit them where it hurts. We know there's one man behind it, and you know I've heard his voice. Clearly, Sharma is a big part of his plans and the gang. *And* he's got experience. A copper's experience. So we take him out of the equation.'

There was a silence. 'You mean – ahem,' started Ranveer, 'you mean?'

'No, no. Of course not. What are you, crazy? No, we don't kill him, we just turn him. Get him to work for us. Then maybe get one of the others after that. If the leader falls short of men, he's bound to try and compensate, and he'll make a mistake. And then, we'll be there to rub his face in the mud.'

Get at the periphery. Get the others out of the way. That'll harm the brain. It'll take time to reboot from its pain, and in that time, when it's not aware of its surroundings, we pounce.

'There's something I don't understand, sir,' said Rahul, looking a little puzzled. 'Why didn't we do this earlier? It would have worked in Chandigarh.'

I sighed. 'My oversight, Rahul. I underestimated them. I thought they were clever and lucky. But the truth is that they're very, *very* clever and cunning, plus really, *really* lucky. We know that now.'

Ranveer got up. 'So what do you want us to do?'

I thought for a full minute before replying. 'Get on the phone. I want the two of you to contact every single major police station in the country. Don't give me those looks, you're paid to do this stuff. Get some men to help you, but I want *your* eyes on the table at all times. They'll strike again, but not very soon.' I remembered the look in Sharma's eyes as he waved to me. It was cocky, cheeky and everything else, but there had also been relief. And that meant we had got really close. 'They'll lie low for a while, but they will strike, believe me.'

I turned to Rahul. 'I also want your report on their escape, but write two. I don't care about the official one, write what you want to and shove it up the AD's ass. I want another one, only for me. You write down everything, and I mean *everything* you saw, did, everyone you noticed, suspicious, routine, the whole jing bang. Leave *nothing* out. There was a hole in their escape plan, and I'm going to find it. That's why I need other perspectives.'

Ranveer got up. 'Okay, sir. And I don't think it will be difficult to trace Sharma and bring him in—'

'No!' I said firmly. Don't bring him in. Let him remain free, but keep a watch over him.'

'But why?' he said, surprised.

'Because we'll need him when they're planning something. If we get him before, they'll know the game's up, and we'll never catch them. Wait for them to plan something, *then* we bring him in. Make him spill on the others, see if we can't turn him to our side and play him against them.'

Rahul nodded. 'Of course. It sounds simple,' he said, getting up and coming over to me. 'You'll get them, sir. This is just temporary.'

I grunted my thanks.

All right, clever boy. Mr X, I'll call you. Mr X who's pulling all the strings and making your three puppets dance. Let's see how clever you are when the ground has been taken out from under you. I'm prepared to wait, the way only cops can wait for a criminal – who can never wait long enough.

You won round one, Mr X, but I'm taking you out in round two. You made a mistake, and it's going to cost you.

As Rahul patched up my mutilated hand, the cool monologue in my brain paused for a few minutes to let my throat do a little screaming.

13

Calcutta Caper

Sharmaji had almost begun to fear Ajay had ditched him for good when his call came through.

'Hello, Sharmaji, how are you?' he said, sounding absolutely normal, the friendly Ajay he had always known.

Sharmaji's voice fawned over Ajay, like a dog with its long-lost master. 'I'm very well, thank you, Ajay! Thanks for calling, yaar. I was so afraid you were never going to talk to me again. I didn't know what to do—'

Ajay interrupted, a little sharply. 'It's done, Sharmaji. Let's put the past behind us. I was thinking that we're becoming a little rusty. Maybe it's time we tried something?'

'Of course, of course! Exactly what I was thinking too!' gasped Sharmaji.

'Good, good. I'll meet you at Chandigarh airport then.'

'When?'

'Soon. You'll know when,' said Ajay and hung up.

Sharmaji put the receiver back on the hook, enormously relieved, and thoughtful. Several things about the call disturbed him, most of all the fact that Ajay had called directly on his landline. Earlier, it would always be a cryptic message, upon which Sharmaji would make a mad dash for the nearest telephone booth and wait for Ajay to call there. But this time, he had called him at his home. And spoken freely. He must know that after their narrow escape, the police would be hot on their tail; the first thing they would do was to bug Sharmaji's house and phone. Strangely, they'd never called on him, never dragged him away for questioning, even after he'd returned home more than two weeks later. That surprised him no end. The police, however lazy they may be, would never give up the hunt if they had a clue to follow. So why were they ignoring him now?

It had been nearly three months since that day. Three months without a word from Ajay. He'd tried several times to get in touch with Ajay, but always got the cold shoulder. He'd been expecting it, of course, especially after the drubbing he'd received that day on the train.

Ajay never shouted. He had this curiously, quiet way of speaking, which was worse than any yelling. And in that soft voice, he had torn Sharmaji to shreds. 'What were you thinking, Sharmaji? Can you really be such a moron?' he'd said, as the train chugged its way to Howrah. They had met just outside the pantry car, since they were in different coaches.

'I thought you were a conman, the best there was. I thought you knew what you were doing. But to show your hand like a rank amateur—'

Sharmaji rebelled. Well, his pride did, at any rate. 'That's unfair, Ajay. Be careful what you say, it won't—'

'You can't threaten me, Sharmaji. You know that. You can't hope to win against me. The least you could have done was to follow my instructions, as you usually do. To the letter. You *can* read, can't you?'

Sharmaji maintained a sullen silence. You really couldn't talk back to a man who'd just taken your warning and thrown it back in your face, with a side helping of his own.

'You've been in this business for more than a decade, and this is what you do? Reveal yourself to a cop who's clever enough to track us down to the station? How do you know he's not tracking us right now? What if *I'm* not clever enough, what if he sees through my plan?'

It had gone on for a while, even Joginder and Iqbal remaining silent. Finally, Ajay said, 'We'll have to stay out of all of this for a while. At least until the heat cools. After we get to Howrah, we'll go our separate ways. Don't contact anyone. Wait two weeks, before you go back home.'

Iqbal spoke. 'What about us? You know, the gang?'

There was steel in Ajay's voice as he replied, 'There might not *be* an "us" much longer. We'll just have to wait and see how much Sharmaji's stupidity has cost us.'

That was the last time they'd spoken. Sharmaji spent the rest of the train ride to Calcutta and the next two weeks there in utter misery and fear of being apprehended. But nothing happened. Then Ajay called abruptly at his hotel, told him to go back home, and hung up. He hadn't even waited for Sharmaji to ask him how he'd found out where the older man was staying. Sharmaji was sure he'd left no tracks, but Ajay always found out. He was a genius, and a small part of Sharmaji was still feeling guilty for letting him down.

He'd gone back home, fully expecting to be hauled to the police station in a matter of hours. But the hours went by, and then the days, and the weeks, and nothing happened. It was too easy.

Now that Ajay had called, they were sure to know about it. But then, knowing Ajay, he would know they were listening too. Then why?

Sharmaji shook his head. Maybe Ajay had some game to play, or maybe he'd just screwed up. He'd have to sort it out later. Right now, it seemed they might be back in business soon.

Two weeks later, Sharmaji met Ajay at the airport. In his usual ingenious way, Ajay had waited until the last moment to tell him when they would be travelling, and even then, the note had come inside the morning newspaper. Not just any paper, the one that Sharmaji alone read in the entire household. How Ajay discovered these killer details was something Sharmaji was content to marvel at, because he never revealed his secrets.

That night, he told his wife that he would be leaving on business for a while, forbidden her to tell anyone about it, prayed that she wouldn't, and left in the dead of night.

Early next morning, they met at the airport. Ajay was waiting for him, concealed beneath one of his disguises; Sharmaji would have completely missed him had he not walked straight into him.

'Nobody followed you,' said Ajay.

'No, I wasn't followed. I kept checking,' replied Sharmaji,

'I know, I wasn't asking. I am telling you.'

He handed the older man a cup of tea, and they sat down on a bench just outside the airport. 'So, where are we going?' said Sharmaji.

'Calcutta,' said Ajay, sipping his tea.

'We're going back there?'

Ajay nodded. 'Yes. Practice runs. And to get some cash flow,' he said, smiling a little ruefully. 'We do need the cash, don't we?'

Sharmaji nodded emphatically.

'Well then.'

'Ajay, I've been meaning to ask you,' started Sharmaji, and paused, fumbling for words.

'Mmm?'

'That day, at the station, inside the toilet. What happened to you? I mean, I couldn't even recognize your voice, and shit! I was really scared, I don't mind telling you!' breathed Sharmaji.

Ajay sighed. 'To tell you the truth, I don't know how I did that. I was all right when I told you guys the plan, I was fine when I hid inside the loo. But when I saw that cop coming in after you, it took everything I had to stop myself running away that very instant.'

He frowned, thinking hard. 'I don't know what happened to me, Sharmaji. My mind wasn't working fully. I had never come up against a cop like that. And this cop was a good one, one of the better ones, I could tell. There was only one way I could get out of there, and that was to convince him that I *would* kill him if he didn't let us go.'

Sharmaji watched as Ajay spoke, mouth half open.

'And then, I had to do something. Even after you left, I couldn't just tell him not to follow us and walk out. I had to take him out. Sharmaji, that was the first time I ever hit another man in cold blood. Did you know that? I had to remind myself not to hit the vertebrae or the brain stem, because that would have killed him. I'd read about it in college, but I'd never thought I'd have a practical exam on it someday!'

'And where did you get the gun?'

Ajay smiled. 'What gun?'

'The gun! That gun you were holding! You threatened to shoot him.'

'No, I didn't threaten to shoot him. I merely suggested that he would be wise not to move. His brain filled in the rest of the fear.'

'And the gun?' Sharmaji persisted.

'Does everything that's cold and pressed up against your back have to be a gun? It could be... I don't know...' Ajay patted his pockets theatrically. 'It could simply be a keychain, or a pipe I ripped off the wall as I waited for you to come in.' He winked.

Sharmaji realized he'd been holding his breath, and let it out with a big whoosh.

'My god, Ajay! Only you could have done something like that.'

Ajay nodded.

'But tell me something. This thing in Calcutta. Is it big?'

'Well, not too big, no.'

'Ajay, you've got to stop this!' said Sharmaji earnestly, getting worked up again. 'Look, I'm getting old. My mind and body and reflexes aren't what they used to be. I want out. One big game, one big shot, and I'm out.'

Ajay was silent.

'The kids are getting older, Ajay. And look what happened at the station. I had a dream last night that my son-in-law was coming to meet me in jail! And you weren't around either!'

Ajay laughed and winked at Sharmaji. 'But I was right there. You didn't see me because I was standing right behind you.'

Sharmaji stared at Ajay, apparently struggling for words. Finally, he broke into a smile. 'Thanks, man.' He slapped the younger man on his back. 'So. Calcutta?'

'Yes.'

'And it's not a big job?'

'We need more men for a big job,' Ajay reminded him. 'And we need more money to keep them.'

'If I'd been working, I would be retiring now,' sniffed Sharmaji gloomily.

'That's what you've been saying for five years.'

Sharmaji looked at him. 'But I'm serious this time.'

Ajay winked at him mischievously. 'That's what you've been saying for *three* years.'

Again, Ajay's infectious mirth won Sharmaji over, and he relaxed. 'Yeah, yeah,' he muttered, complaining but only half-heartedly now. 'Kids these days…'

Ajay dug into his pocket, and brought out a brown paper bag. 'Here you go, Sharmaji. Tickets and money. For you, Iqbal and Joginder. I'll meet you there directly.'

Sharmaji peered inside the bag. The contents had a cheering effect on him.

The two of them got up. 'I'll tell you one thing,' said Ajay, leaning in closer. 'You're right. I am planning something. But not right now. It'll be big. Just another couple of rounds, and we'll be done.'

Sharmaji smiled again.

The following week, the four of them met in New Market, at Calcutta's famous Baadshah restaurant.

Joginder and Iqbal had arrived just the day before. They had purposely chosen a slow route out of the station, in a rickshaw that took them through the winding streets of Bada Bazar.

They conferred in quiet voices.

'Seems okay, not much security… '

'They're all small traders, so they won't have too much…'

'What do you mean, they won't have too much?'

'The police aren't around much, I didn't see any patrols… '

'The police station is not very far, but they're a really sleepy bunch… '

'…not too much? Does that mean they'll have too little?'

'I've booked us a car for the day. No questions asked…'

'We'll have to do it quickly, if the police station is nearby…'

'...how little are we talking about...'

'It won't be a problem. In fact, we'll get them to help, like at Minister Gupta's house...'

'Of course! They'll never suspect...'

'I've got the radio, we'll be listening in on their frequency too...'

'We'll hit three or four, not many...'

'...and a four-way share means even less...'

'We'll pack up the whole thing in an hour, not more.'

Ajay nodded at Iqbal, who got up, gathered his knapsack and entered the loo in the restaurant. A minute later, a total stranger emerged and went out the front door.

Joginder too got up, changed inside the loo and left, winking at Ajay.

'How little, Ajay?' asked Sharmaji, still anxious.

'Don't worry. It'll be enough. Now go change. I'll pay the bill.'

Ajay was already in disguise, and was probably the only person out of the four emerging from Baadshah who looked his usual self. They bundled into the car Ajay had booked, and left.

Target: Bada Bazar.

Fate had a surprise for them at the very first store.

As the four arrived at Poddar Traders in Bada Bazar, looking even more officious than actual officials and with a posse of policemen behind them, they heard a sound they'd never encountered before. As they barged into the shop, they realized, a little too late, what that sound was.

The shop was already being raided.

All activity ceased, men around the shop frozen in various postures as Sharmaji, in the lead, skidded to a halt, the others behind him. There was a thunderous silence.

Sharmaji managed to find his voice. He also managed, barely, to keep the squeak out of it. 'Who are you?'

The man leading the raid frowned in obvious puzzlement. 'Income tax. Who are *you*?'

This time, Sharmaji was zapped. His voice lost itself in the recesses of his throat as his brain slunk into some unknown corner.

Just behind him were Ajay, Iqbal and Joginder. None of them, not even Ajay, had been prepared for such an eventuality.

Images of jails and prison clothes and bending down to pick up soap flashed through Joginder's mind. He glanced back at the four real Calcutta policemen standing behind him, and saw the first signs of suspicion dawn on their faces.

Very slowly, the cop leading the four reached down and unhooked his holster's catch.

It was all over, thought Iqbal. All because of a fucking coincidence. He waited to hear someone say the words he'd never thought he'd have to hear: I surrender.

The words never came. Barely two seconds had gone by when Ajay stepped forward. 'Income tax? You're from the income tax department?' There was, if nothing else, authority in his voice. It was a voice, everyone subconsciously nodded to themselves, that was used to command.

Ajay turned to Sharmaji. 'Show me the papers.'

The still slack-jawed Sharmaji looked at Ajay through glazed eyes. 'Uuurgh?' he said.

'The papers, man!' said Ajay sharply. 'You have the raid order, right?'

His voice snapped the older man back to the present. 'Hem, y-y-yes, sir. Um... here you go?' he said, handing over a cash memo from a sweet shop.

Ajay gazed at the paper intently, brows furrowed. Then he looked up at the income-tax fellow. 'Agarwal Traders?'

The man shook his head. 'Poddar Traders.'

'124?'

'214.'

His face black as thunder, Ajay swivelled back to Sharmaji again. 'What the hell is this?' he yelled. It took a moment for the startled trio to realize that he was actually speaking Bengali, and another for them to wonder how in hell he could have learned it.

Finally, Sharmaji pulled his beleaguered mind together. In the face of Ajay's onslaught, he had to look appropriately shamefaced, and he managed now.

But Ajay wasn't done. 'Can't you even check the number properly, you old fool? I'll lose my job because of your fucking stupidity!'

'Sorry, sir.'

'Now you've disturbed these gentlemen. Maybe it's time for you to retire your old ass!'

Iqbal and Joginder barely managed to suppress their smirks.

The income-tax team's leader stepped in, just then. Clearly, Ajay's harsh words and Sharmaji's dejected appearance had made a gentler man out of him. 'It ij all right,' he said sympathetically, in that thick accent unique to Bengalis. 'Mishtake happen shomtimes.'

Ajay turned to him, and said in fluent Bengali, 'I'm so sorry for the trouble. Please continue, we'll be out of your hair immediately.' He threw Sharmaji a dirty look. 'We've got our jobs to do too.'

Ajay held out his hand, and they shook. There were smiles all around.

Ajay left with his men and the Calcutta police personnel, nobody the wiser. They had managed to outwit even the official raiders.

Within fifteen minutes, they were in a different part of Bada Bazar, unfazed as they paid visits to scared businessmen. Sharmaji happily returned to his bluster, slapping people left and right. The four of them, aided by the able police force they had assembled, raided five shops and recovered black money from each of them. And just as they had done before, the police helped them pack everything into the car, signed a couple of papers and watched as the four left in different vehicles, waiting expectantly for the call from their police station: a call that would never come.

The waiter at the Baadshah vaguely remembered that four men had come a few hours ago for lunch, similar to the men who now sat eating snacks. He didn't have time to pay much attention to them, he didn't notice the empty gunny bags they had dumped under the table as they ate.

What the waiter remembered was the generous tip.

Ajay wasn't done with Calcutta just yet. There was one more trip, one more target. He briefed them as they drove towards south Calcutta.

'Customs officer?' Joginder cried, nearly ramming into the car in front of them, in his astonishment.

Ajay nodded. 'Not to worry, I've done my homework. He's one of the most bent officers around.'

'Nononono, Ajay, let's not do this,' moaned Sharmaji. 'First we almost get caught, just as we return to work, and now you want to take an even bigger risk?'

Ajay didn't say anything, just smiled his secretive smile.

'And since when did we become income-tax officers, eh?' demanded Sharmaji, finally finding his tongue regarding the morning's near-faux pas.

Joginder and Iqbal pricked up their ears.

'You should have seen your face, Sharmaji!' said Ajay, a twinkle in his eye.

Iqbal and Joginder burst out laughing at the sight of Sharmaji's big, red, indignant face.

'Don't muck about, Ajay. What if that man had asked to see the raid order? You're going to get us killed someday, I'm telling you!'

Ajay shrugged. 'I saved you today, didn't I!'

Iqbal interrupted. 'But you know, Ajay, I'm a little worried about this next one too.'

'Yes!' said Sharmaji, at last finding support. 'See, they're both worried!'

'Don't worry, you guys. It'll be a walk in the park.'

'Hmph,' said Sharmaji. 'Anyway, I've had enough for today. You lead this one.'

Which Ajay did. It was amazing, really, how he slipped from the role of Sharmaji's helper to the raiding team leader. At Assistant Commissioner (Customs) Shounak Ghosh's plush house in south Calcutta, he seemed to be charged with an inexplicable energy, and there was a gleam in his eyes that the others had never seen before.

Everything went as planned, just as before. Easier, actually, as Ghosh was stone drunk, and could barely stand. The sight of CBI officers turning his house upside down – finding all the goods he had never thought anyone would find – sobered him up somewhat, but by that time, Ajay had him completely under control.

'You've g-g-got it w-w-rong,' he mumbled feebly. 'I'm an honest man, I—'

Ajay grabbed his collar and threw him against the wall. Then he spoke quietly.

Sharmaji once again heard the voice he'd heard inside the toilet in Ludhiana, and it sent a shiver down his spine. 'Say what you want, deny all you want, but say one more time that you're honest, and I'll knock a hole through your head. With this hammer.'

Ghosh locked his mouth and threw away the key. He wasn't *that* drunk.

Ten minutes later, they left him on the floor muttering to himself, holding a piece of paper that Ajay had made him sign. The raid was officially a success.

Back in the car, the unspoken question hung in the air, until Joginder, after a lot of clearing of his throat, gave voice to it. 'Ajay, why the anger? He was just another crooked guy!'

For a while, Ajay didn't reply. Then he said quietly, 'It was personal. Because of him, I once didn't get a job.' But he refused to say anything more.

14

The First Breakthrough

Three months. Three fucking months, and not a peep out of those bastards. I was beginning to wonder whether Rahul and Ranveer were doing what I'd told them to. I went over to their room, which they'd converted into their own personal HQ within the HQ. I found them among piles of files and paper and wastepaper baskets and unfinished meals. They didn't even have the time to speak to me; clearly they were focussing on our mission. I hurried back out.

Where the hell are you, Mr X? You're not a common criminal, are you? Most others thieving like you would have raised their ugly ass heads by now, and I would have happily lopped them off. Metaphorically, of course. But you, no, you seem to be something else altogether. Why would you go to earth like this when nobody's chasing you? Sharmaji may have told you how we cops work, so you know the heat is off sooner than you think. So where's your move, chum?

It seemed like I was finally up against a worthy adversary. I'd spent years chasing after gangsters and crooks, all of them far more dangerous and deadly than this bloke. Their names were in the papers, men affiliated to the likes of Haji Mastan, Varadarajan Mudaliar and other mafia bosses. These were my targets, and truth to tell, none of them had any brains. Or finesse. Not like Mr X.

But wait! There was another possibility. What if he was running scared? Mr X and his gang had been around for quite a while, hitting crooked traders and politicians and actors. Nobody had come close to catching them. Except me. And I had gotten really close. Maybe that had scared the X-Men off.

Fuck, I hoped not! These people could make my career, set it on an irreversible upward spiral. I needed the X-Men.

The phone rang, managing to sound desperately urgent. I looked at it with distaste, wishing it would stop, allowing me to go back to my daydreaming. Many a crime had been solved because of an epiphany while aimlessly mooching about at work.

But the damn thing kept ringing. Sighing, I picked up the receiver. And was instantly alert. The call was from my friend Kalyan Banerjee, a deputy commissioner with the crime branch of the Calcutta Police.

After I had told Rahul and Ranveer to check with all the police stations in the whole damn country, it had occurred to me that said task was Herculean in nature, and might need some support on the side. So I'd tapped into the old boys' network, buzzed all my old friends and acquaintances from my early IPS days, and told them to let me know if they heard something about the wraiths I was chasing.

And here was Banerjee, handing me a trail to the ghosts. 'You got lucky.'

'What do you mean?'

'Four men raided three shops in Bada Bazar this morning. Of course, by three, I mean the three that are telling. There may be more who've clammed up.'

'CBI?'

'Yep. All the traders work in grey areas, have pots and pots of black money stashed away. These boys of yours are really doing you a favour.'

'Fuck that, don't remind me. And don't tell me you're not pissed off. They're fooling *your* men into helping them raid the goddamn place!'

Banerjee chuckled. 'It's bloody amusing, I tell you. You should see the faces of my men!'

I'd always thought the man had a weird sense of humour. 'Anyway, they're filing an FIR now, but we're having a hard time keeping it quiet—'

'Quiet?' I shouted. 'Absolutely not! *Don't* keep it quiet, man! We've tiptoed long enough around these bastards. I want the news out, I want every damn newspaper in the country to get it.'

He paused a second before replying, 'And what about the FIR?'

'I don't care about the FIR, Banerjee. Do what you will. But I want the news in tomorrow's paper. And it has to be printed big and bold.'

'All right,' he said. 'I'll see what I can do.'

I hung up just as Ranveer put his head around the door. 'Sir, I think we've got a hit, but I'm not sure.'

I waved him in, and yelled, 'Rahul!'

He arrived immediately, as usual unamused by my yelling out to him rather than using the intercom.

'All right, Ranveer, what do you have?'

'Like I said, sir, I'm not sure. There was a raid at some shop in a place called—' He squinted at a piece of paper.

I steepled my hands in front of my face and looked at him over the fingertips. 'Bada Bazar,' I said.

He looked up quickly. 'How did you know?'

'I got a call from an old friend. I know. Same as before. Four men, CBI raid, police—'

Rahul interrupted. 'Not CBI, income tax.'

I sat up. 'Are you sure?'

He nodded.

Now this was puzzling. Banerjee had said CBI. These guys always posed as the CBI. Then why the income-tax department, now? Of course, the IT fellows were robbers too, but they hid behind desks and policies and the law. This meant that there could be *another* group of men with the *same* modus operandi. A statistical impossibility, my brain told me. Which could only mean that the IT raid was for real. And if it was, maybe...

I looked at Ranveer. 'Do you have the details?'

He nodded.

'All right. The IT raid was in Bada Bazar?'

'Yes.'

'Then maybe they know about some other raid in the same vicinity.'

A look of doubt crept onto Rahul's face. 'Are you sure, sir? It seems a stretch...'

I nodded, not looking at him. 'I know it's a long shot. But we have to try something. The news of the robbery will be out in every newspaper tomorrow. It'll scare the gang. Meanwhile, the more information we can get on them, the better. We'll have more ammo, and they'll be scared. Better chances of catching them.'

Rahul looked doubtful, but didn't protest.

Ranveer was still standing, looking from Rahul to me. 'Get onto the IT guys who held the raid,' I told him. 'I want all details on their raid, and if they saw or noticed anyone else. They may not remember anything, but every little bit counts.'

Long shots only work in movies, when the hero has just a few seconds left to escape a horrific death, or when the detective needs inspiration and his obliging imagination hands him one. It doesn't happen in real life – a motto I've always lived by.

Well, there are always exceptions.

Within half an hour, the IT guys had told us about the other party who'd stumbled into their raid, said they'd got the wrong address and hurried away. They told us that the men were followed by the Calcutta Police. They then gave us the most stupendous lead we'd got in the case yet – descriptions of the gang members. Well, most of them, at any rate.

'Yeah, I know the leader is a fat bastard with a moustache. He's an ex-cop. What else?' I asked the man who had led the IT team, a man called Ghoshal.

'You're... er... mistaken, Mr Khan,' Ghoshal said. 'The fat one was a lackey. The leader was much younger.'

This was new. And significant. 'Younger?' I said, trying to keep the excitement from my voice.

'Yes, around twenty-five or twenty-six,' he said. 'Yelled at the... em... fat bastard for bringing him to the wrong address.'

'What did he look like?'

'Medium build, close-cropped hair, clean shaven, spectacles, thinnish, I'd call him. He was wearing a blue checked shirt with black trousers.'

Impressive, I thought. Only, he'd described about 40 per cent of the Indian population. Anyway, now we knew one crucial thing. Mr X was a young man. And where there are young leaders, there are bound to be unhappy middle-aged men pissed off at being lorded over. That gave us an advantage, a hook to pull in Sharma and use him against the gang. Plus, of course, a young leader would surround himself with young folk. Which meant that there was a high probability the other two in the gang were also around the same age.

I left the 'thank you for your information, it was most helpful' job to Rahul. I had to think. I needed a plan.

The next week was spent in hectic, indeed frenzied research. This time, all three of us — Rahul, Ranveer and myself — were working, instead of the two of them doing the grinding stuff and me doing the thinking. We were looking for a link.

We dug into Sharma's file again and this time, we went through all his known acquaintances with increased attention. Everything after Sharma's suspension for trying to take a bribe was hauled up. Somewhere along the way, we would find Mr X. It was straightforward, logical common sense. If you look hard enough, you'll find what you're looking for.

Unfortunately, nobody seemed to have informed logic or common sense, because nearly a week went by without any of us being the wiser. We dug deeper, went further into the past, but all it showed us was the opposite of what we were looking for. The man Sharma, even during his tenure with the police force, had mixed with his peers, not with those above him, nor with those below. And almost all of his peers were of his age, or thereabouts. Nobody even came close to the description we had got from the IT man.

Maybe the son of a friend, or a nephew. But no, again we drew a blank. Sharma didn't have any nephews, and the only young acquaintance he had was the son of one of his former colleagues in the force. We had just begun to feel lucky when we discovered that the kid had been killed in a motorcycle accident.

Nothing, *nothing* suggested that Sharma had even met a youth, let alone allowed him to join his gang. The gentle grilling of his family during the wedding had revealed nothing. Of course, there were hundreds of dove-eyed idiots mooning about like they always do at weddings, but it was not just difficult to identify a genius criminal mastermind among them, it was impossible.

After a week, I left the work to the indomitable Rahul and Ranveer, and finally went home.

Shazia had just returned from Bombay, where she had gone to visit her aunt. She was always insisting that we move to Bombay, and that I should apply for a transfer, and now as usual she was filled with the charm of that city and its fast life and opportunities. 'I'm telling you, darling,' she would say, 'you should tell them to send you to Bombay. Then you'll see what life is like. Oh, the people there are so friendly, and they're all so energetic…' She would go on for a while, quite forgetting that she loved Delhi, loved its old-world charm, the wide roads, its many romantic, historic settings.

This time, too, was no different. She had returned full of stories, and I ate my dinner listening to her talk of how beautiful the sunset was on Marine Drive.

Maybe it was the lingering excitement of Bombay, or perhaps she had been missing me, but that night, she came to me hot and willing, seducing me like she used to just after our marriage. Not many people went against their families to marry, but we had, and had never regretted it for a moment. But however deep our love remained, the fires of passion needed constant rekindling, and tonight I saw her fully kindled.

I didn't wait for us to get to bed. I didn't wait for us to undress. Snatching her up in my arms, I bore her to the divan, her hands clawing at my shirt's buttons. My hand wormed her way into her blouse and settled around her soft breasts; then I ripped her blouse open, finally revealing her ample bosom, the pain from the broken wrist worth every second of the blissful sight, the feel of her naked body against mine.

We were both breathing heavily as I massaged her breast with one hand, the other sliding down slowly towards her navel. There it found unfamiliarity, and stopped. 'What's this?' I asked.

'It's a silver waist chain,' she gasped. 'I got it from Zaveri Bazar, Bombay.'

'Let's get it off, my love,' I said, fumbling with the damn thing. Nothing like a useless piece of jewellery blocking the journey of your lust, dampening your libido.

'You know, we should really move to Bombay,' she said, moaning as my fingers caressed her naked skin. Skin that hardly saw the light of day. 'You can go there for the CBI. They're hiring…' Her voice trailed off as I kneaded her skin, my fingers almost at—

'The CBI hiring?' I said, temporarily baffled.

She had thrown her head back in pleasure. 'My brother told me. They're hiring men for the CBI in Bombay. Maybe you should apply again, and ask for a posting in Bombay.'

Something was wrong. It nagged at the back of my mind like an unscratchable itch. I shrugged it away. Shazia's hands were moving towards my trousers and undoing my belt. It was flung aside, and her hand slowly moved further...

I froze. She felt my body stiffen, and stopped herself. 'What is it?'

'The CBI. Hiring in Bombay. Where did your brother hear that?'

My heart was beating faster as she answered, and it wasn't because of the blood rushing the way it had been heading these last few minutes. 'It was in some newspaper.' She frowned. 'Why?'

Damn. Sometimes, I hated having the brain of a cop. 'Darling,' I said, getting up, 'the CBI doesn't hire. They recruit. Through exams, training, and more exams. The best get through.'

My wife looked bewildered, and infuriated. 'And that's why you're getting up? Leaving me here like this?'

Uh oh. Here we go, again. 'I'm so sorry, my love. But I promise you, if all goes well, if I catch these bastards I'm after, we'll go to Bombay.'

She gave me a look of disbelief, sat up slowly and started buttoning up her blouse. 'You'd better go. I know that look. You won't stop until you get them.'

They say few men can achieve anything without the support of a woman. Looking at Shazia, I couldn't agree more.

My mind was still half full of her as I reached the office, a fact made apparent by Ranveer, who pointed out that my fly was open. But as I revealed my hunch, the case slowly filled to take up every available space in my head.

'Rahul, get onto the grapevine on the double. First find out if the CBI does put out such advertisements in newspapers, which I'm sure they don't!' The idea was laughable. By the time I'd got my cup of coffee and returned to my desk, he was back, smiling.

'They're all laughing, sir,' he replied to my quizzical look. 'The CBI doesn't work like that, they said.'

I sat down at my desk and said, 'Anything else?'

Clearly, from Ranveer's face as he stared out of the window, avoiding both Rahul's eyes and mine, there had been a lot more.

Being the faithful men they were, both Rahul and Ranveer shook their heads. 'No, nothing much, sir,' Rahul said, his face wooden.

'Hmm. Well, anyway, that was just to confirm. So A, the CBI didn't put out that ad. B, that means that someone else did. C, that means that someone did something illegal. D, we find out who it is.'

I was going to go through a few more alphabets, but Ranveer interrupted. 'Sir, while Rahul was checking up on… ahem… anyway, I called a friend of mine in Bombay, told him to check the ad.'

He looked down at his notepad, which went everywhere with him. 'This is what it says,' he said, and handed me the pad.

'Wanted 50 dynamic graduates for intelligence officers post and security officers post. Males and Females. Come personally for interview with bio-data, certificates, passport size photo at Holiday Inn Hotel enquiry counter between 10 a.m. and 5 p.m. on Thursday.'

'When was this?' I asked.

'Sunday. Yesterday, sir,' Ranveer said, apparently needing to explain further. 'Of course, now it's Tuesday, but—'

Rahul shushed him into silence with a look. I continued staring at the ad.

It *couldn't* be a coincidence. It just couldn't. It was too pat, too well-timed. But they were talking about the CBI, which was at the centre of Mr X's MO. So what the hell did it all mean?

I turned to Rahul. 'The two of you, take two men and fly out to Bombay. Immediately. The ad says Thursday, that's day after tomorrow. So you have one day. Get on the first flight to Bombay and use your instincts. You know how I'm thinking, you've been with this case from the start. Try to think like the leader.'

Ranveer interrupted. 'Yes, sir, but what do you want us to do?'

'I want you to stake out as many places as you can think of where the gang might hit. Take some men from here, but when you get there, get some local cops behind you. Get them to tell you the sensitive spots, the smaller traders who look small but deal big. That's the gang's MO. That's where they'll hit.'

Rahul nodded, his face rapt with attention. Ranveer, on the other hand, looked dumbfounded. 'Sir, Bombay is huge! How can just a few of us—'

I put my hand on his shoulder. 'Son, I told you you'd get your opportunity to prove yourself. Well, here's your first. Use your brains, put yourself in their place, and take a few guesses. You've studied their hits, figure it out.'

'But won't you come?'

'I'll come. But first, I have to read up on all of this. You guys get there and start work. I'll join you in the afternoon.'

Rahul got up. 'When do we leave, sir?'

I had just picked up the phone and was dialling as I answered. 'Well, I'm calling the chief now for permission, so in another half hour.'

Everything about the operation was one big guess. An educated guess, of course, born of years of instinctual thinking, now honed to near perfection. When I arrived in Bombay the next evening and went to the rendezvous site, I expected some results.

Apparently, I'd underestimated the situation.

I'd just settled into the makeshift HQ in Worli police camp when Ranveer and Rahul walked in. Both of them looked as if they'd had a long, hard, tiring, but in the end fruitful day.

Rahul spoke. 'I think we've got him, sir.'

I didn't say anything. No point jumping to conclusions without getting the full picture.

'We cased almost all of the city, from yesterday morning. We contacted the CBI's city unit, and they in turn mobilized the local police.'

'Ah. Solanki, isn't it?'

'No, sir. Solanki's retired.'

About time. 'I see. So who's in charge now?'

'Solanki.'

There was a pause.

'Not my fault if they have the same name,' Rahul grumbled under his breath.

Ranveer coughed an interruption. 'Hmm, by the way, sir, I thought there was a lot of jurisdiction nonsense in such cases, bad blood and all?'

I nodded. 'There is. If people from another state come to your place and try to lord it over you and call you incompetent, I doubt you'd want to invite them in for a nice cold one.'

'Then how…?'

'I have friends, Ranveer. I scratch their back, they scratch mine. I told them my men needed some assistance and a hurdle-free path.'

Rahul nodded. 'I thought as much. Well, whoever your friends are, sir, please tell them we appreciate their help. It would've been a lot more difficult without them.'

I nodded, then gestured impatiently. 'All right, what do you have?'

Rahul took an envelope out of his bag and deposited it on the table in front of me. 'Photographs, sir. At a jeweller's shop in a place called Zaveri Bazar. The jewellers in that area are some of the biggest in the city. I was there this afternoon. Last evening, I called that income-tax guy again in Calcutta, and got him to fax me a rough sketch of the man he saw.'

He handed me the sketch. Then he pulled out some photographs from the envelope. 'Check it out, sir.'

I held up the sketch and the photo and compared them. It might *just* be the one. In fact, it *had* to be the one. Either the sketch artist was good, or the IT fellow had insisted on the details, but whatever it was, the bloke in the photograph was even wearing the same shirt as in the sketch. And he fit. He certainly fit the description.

Finally. A part of my brain switched off its lights and went to bed. It was the part that kept supplying the rest with imaginary figures. Now there was no more need for it. I have a face for you, Mr X. All I need now is a name.

I knew it was highly improbable, but I tried anyway. 'Do we have a name?' I said, not taking my eyes off the photo.

Out of the corner of my eye, I saw Ranveer shake his head. 'No, sir. I checked all records, went through everything we have. I can confirm that we've never met this guy before.'

Oh well, guess you'll have to be Mr X a little longer, chum. I'm here now, and I'm on your tail.

There was that nagging feeling again, and I realized soon what it was. But it was Rahul who gave voice to it.

'Sir,' he said, scratching his head apologetically. 'If this fellow is as brainy as he seems, why would he make such an obvious mistake?'

I'd been hoping nobody would ask that. But then these *were* my men. Naturally they'll think of everything between them.

I shook my head. 'The human mind is a strange thing, Rahul. Give it some panic and a lot of food for thought, and sooner or later, it's bound to make a mistake.'

Both Rahul and Ranveer nodded. The words certainly *seemed* plausible enough.

Unknown (hopefully) to the two, I too had my reservations. This guy was such a genius that he'd been with Sharma god knows how long and had the much older ex-cop eating out of his hand. At just twenty-six or twenty-seven years of age, he had outwitted a senior, veteran cop. So why would someone like that make the elementary mistake of going to a high-stakes area wearing what he'd been last identified in? It almost seemed as if he was *letting* himself be recognized!

I shrugged the thought away the moment it came to me. No way. I was not going to go down that road, the steady downhill climb of paranoia. If you started believing one thing, you'd start believing in half a dozen other things that didn't deserve consideration. Best to wait for cold hard facts.

Maybe the brilliance had paled just the slightest bit, and a crack had shown through. That was all I needed.

I nodded to the photo in my hand. You've made a mistake, pal. Now it's your move again. We'll see who has the last laugh.

15

Planning the Con

It's always unsettling to sit in front of a calm, composed and totally self-assured man. At least, it is for most people.

The man sitting in the chair was feeling unsettled. Of course, the supremely uncomfortable high chair didn't help at all.

He sat as still as he could, trying to emanate confidence. It didn't fool the only other man in the room. It wouldn't even have fooled a newborn who'd just opened his eyes.

Ajay sat on the other side of the table, totally occupied by the sheaf of papers in front of him, apparently reading them with great concentration. He certainly seemed to have forgotten all about the nervous man in front of him, who was trying to gauge what Ajay might be like from what he saw.

The first thing he saw was that Ajay was well dressed. He wore black trousers and a cream shirt, with the collar open and the button at the top undone. His hair was parted on the right and neatly brushed back, and his close-shaven face was smooth and unblemished. His shoes were highly polished and he sat with his legs crossed. He was probably in his early thirties. Despite the chill, he seemed totally at ease.

Breaking the silence seemed like a very bad idea, like poking a stick at a lion that's waiting to pounce. So the nervous man kept quiet and tried to study his surroundings as surreptitiously as he could.

He was in a hall. A big one. One of those fancy, high-ceilinged halls where you could hear the smallest indiscretion from across the room. It was sparsely furnished, if you could describe a 50-by-50 foot room containing just a table and two chairs on either end as furnished. Big door, the high windows. Airy and bright, no doubt about it. Cold as hell.

Feeling even more intimidated, the nervous man looked back at Ajay, and shivered as he saw that he was being subjected to a keen scrutiny. Measured. Sized up.

The man couldn't hold the intensity of that calm, liquid gaze, and looked down. At the papers strewn on the table. They all bore the seal of either the Government of India or the Central Bureau of Investigation.

Knowing they were not for his eyes, the man panicked, and his eyes darted back up. To return to that same cool gaze. What the hell was he supposed to do with his eyes, shut them? Gouge them out? What?

He tried to smile, and felt his face rearrange itself into a pained grimace.

Ajay spoke.

'Why are you here?'

It was a voice of velvet. A male equivalent of Lata Mangeshkar, only with a hidden menace lurking just beneath.

The man's grimace changed to uncomprehending terror. He knew he would give up anything this man asked for; it was what he might ask that terrified him.

'S-s-s-sorry, sir?'

'Why do you want to join the Bureau?'

Now that was a question he was ready for. He had spent the entire morning rehearsing just the perfect answer for that question. Yes, he would kill this test!

'Sir, India is great. Myself Santosh Mane, sir. India is my mother. India is corrupt. I want to…' His brain finally caught up with his mouth. What the hell? That wasn't what he had practised.

His interviewer had arched one eyebrow. It was more frightening than standing in the path of an approaching train.

'Sorry, sir. Sir, there is a lot of corruption in our country, sir. The entire system is in a mess, sir. India's enemies are wringing her dry, sir,' he managed to blurt out.

'So?'

Now he was panicking. Of course he hadn't expected the CBI interview to be easy, but this! This was beyond what he'd imagined. Atlas held up the world, but he felt he was holding up Atlas and the world and the solar system and whatever the hell else there was in the universe.

'S-s-s-so, sir, I want to stop those bastards, sir!'

There was that damned eyebrow again. It danced a knuckle-duster's pattern against his mind.

'You're going to stop them?' The interviewer seemed amused.

Feeling reckless at the encouraging tone, the man said, 'Sir, we'll do it together, sir!'

'And what do you think you'll get out of it?'

It was, the man felt, a loaded question. Was he talking about money? He decided to take a chance. 'Some for you, sir, and some for me…' His voice trailed off.

Ajay raised his hand. The interviewee clamped his mouth shut.

He watched as the other man referred to the paper in front of him again. He glanced through four pages, and finally looked back up at the interviewee.

This time, the man held his gaze, frozen in anticipation.

Then Ajay smiled.

Relief flooded through the man as he grasped that smile and pulled himself out of the quicksand of anxiety.

'Welcome to the CBI, Mr Mane.'

The nervous man stood up and beamed at his interviewer. He felt he should say something, but he was damned if he knew what. 'Thank you, sir. Thank you! Many, many thanks.'

'Yes, yes. You're welcome. Please be here tomorrow, Mr Mane, at ten a.m. sharp.'

'Yes, sir. Of course, sir. I'll be here, sir. I won't be late. Thank you, sir.' The nervous man almost bowed in his relief.

'Good. The door is right behind you. Could you show the next man in on your way out?'

'Of course, sir! I shall tell him, sir. Thank you, sir.'

The nervous man tried to stand up, realized he had already stood up without knowing it, turned and almost ran to the door. There, he checked himself in time, opened it carefully and walked out. The door closed on the silent hall with its lone occupant.

There were several more left to interview. Ajay smiled to himself. Most of them seemed promising.

It would be a long day. But he hoped it would be interesting.

The candidates were all standard fare.

'I want to join the CBI because I want to do good in my country.'

'...I want to put an end to corruption.'

'...I've always been intelligent.'

'...I couldn't get another job.'

'...I am always very honest. Because I want to do something for my country. I love my country.'

'...Peoples wanted to be become filmstar, cricketer, I want to be become Intelligence.'

The gang was spoilt for choice.

Not the most riveting day he'd had. The men who'd come to be interviewed for a 'job' in the country's most elite investigation agency weren't exactly a cross section of the country's most intelligent. There were a few who hovered dangerously near a three-figure IQ, but ultimately didn't pose a problem.

All of them had onc thing in common. None of them stopped to wonder and, even if they did, to actually ask, why the CBI was recruiting men through an advertisement in the newspaper.

The idea had started mostly as a joke. Sharmaji had been pestering Ajay to set his sights higher, play a really big con. And Ajay had been constantly laughing it off, mostly because of the manpower it would require. This wasn't something he was prepared to do. He wasn't going to hire downright crooks. He was fine with people who were a little bent but had their hearts in the right place, as long as they knew to back off when they saw a line they shouldn't cross. But there were some people who either didn't know about such lines or if they did, didn't care about them. These were the hardened criminals, the people who were almost as bad as the politicians and the corrupt people in power. Ajay would *never* work with them, he was clear about that.

He was perfectly happy with the three others in the gang. None of them was really evil. Joginder had been a poor kid on the streets who was forced to turn pickpocket to make ends meet. As they had found out soon after recruiting him, he refused to get drawn into full-fledged thievery, despite his obvious skills and dexterity. In fact, he'd refused to join Ajay and Sharmaji until he'd been persuaded that they would only steal from those who could afford it and deserved it.

Iqbal, however, had been a different matter. He had turned up one day at the garage where Ajay was working at the time, and asked for a job. He was decent with his hands and at the work too, as he soon showed his employers. But he was a strange man, an opinion shared by everyone else who worked in the garage. He was a loner, and hardly spoke. If asked a question, he would reply in monosyllables – saying as much as possible in as few words as was possible – then get back to work. He didn't treat anyone with disrespect; it was not as though he behaved as if he didn't care what the others thought. It was just that he wanted to keep a distance because that was the only way he knew to live.

Within a few weeks, Ajay knew there was more to it. From his vantage point on the first floor of the garage, he could see the entire floor below him, and he observed Iqbal toiling away unquestioningly, unwaveringly. His instinct told him that Iqbal had more to hide than he was letting on. And so, one Friday, when he was getting ready to go to the bank, Ajay paused where Iqbal was sitting, morosely drinking a cup of tea, and asked him to accompany him. It took Ajay not even half the distance to the bank to break through Iqbal's defences and uncover his struggles growing up in poverty; his father's reputation as a gambler, whore-lover and robber; how he'd tried to get job after job but was turned away for being the son of a man with such a black reputation. He'd even applied for a job with the police force, although without much hope. To his surprise, he was rejected not because his father was on the wrong side of the law, but because he was too quiet a person. No aggression, he was told. It took all of a minute for Ajay to convince him that the reason must have been something else, another minute to tell him how he had been given the boot himself, and thirty more seconds to completely win him over with the plan he'd been working on with Sharmaji.

With Joginder, the circle was closed. Ajay didn't want anyone else. But Sharmaji did. He believed that Ajay was gifted enough to play the really big cons. So, as they sat in Ajay's flat in Dongri, Bombay, a few days after the Calcutta heists, he brought up the topic again. Not surprisingly, Iqbal and Joginder joined him in support.

Ajay looked at each of them in turn. 'All of you really think that's what we should do?'

In answer, Sharmaji brought out a crumpled newspaper from his bag and smoothed it open on the table. Written in bold across the front page was the headline: 'Daring Gang Poses As Cops, Pulls Off Heists'.

'That's why we should, Ajay,' he said, jabbing at the headline. 'They're on to us now. They know what we're doing, and how we're doing it. It's only a matter of time before they catch up.'

'So you should be telling me to stop all this, Sharmaji,' said Ajay, frowning. 'But you're telling me the opposite. You're asking me to do something even bigger!'

Sharmaji nodded. 'Yes. And I'll tell you why. Because you can, I know you can, and I want to see you do it and prove me right. And because this will be our last job.'

He got up and started pacing agitatedly. 'You know I'm not as young as I used to be. My mind doesn't work as fast it used to. My reflexes are slower.' He stopped and turned to the others. 'I'm not young, boys. I've married off four daughters now. Soon, they'll all go away. And then it'll only be the missus and me. I want to have a life with her again.'

He slumped down on the chair. 'I-I'm afraid, Ajay,' he said, staring at the floor. 'I'm afraid of screwing up and spending the rest of my life behind bars. Before, it was all adrenalin, excitement, the thrill, the risk... Now, it's all gone. Now, all I have left is the fear.'

That was the moment Ajay made up his mind. He'd never thought Sharmaji would make it up for him – he'd always thought he'd go out when he wanted to. But looking at Sharmaji, he realized the truth of what he was saying. Maybe it *was* time to stop. Maybe Sharmaji was right. If he made a mistake, especially with the cop he suspected was on his tail, he wouldn't live to see a day outside of a prison. Neither would any of them. And of course, it meant he would never see Priya again...

'I understand, Sharmaji,' he said, patting the older man on his shoulder. 'Maybe you're right. I brought you here for something slightly bigger than what we've been doing, but now, come to think of it, we might just raise the stakes even higher.'

He paused, thoughtful. Then he looked around at the others. 'I'll get us something big. Really big. At least a crore.'

There was a collective gasp. 'A cr-crore?' stammered Iqbal. Till now, the most they'd lifted had been six lakh rupees in Madras – and, of course, eleven lakhs in Ludhiana. This last gig had been their biggest ever, they knew. That was in January 1987. The biggest known gang robbery record was still held by Dawood Ibrahim, who, with around seven or eight men, had made away with four lakh seventy-five thousand rupees almost a decade earlier. Of course, few knew of Ajay's gang's antics, and he liked to keep it that way. So a six lakh, or even a ten lakh figure meant an astronomical sum for the gang. And here was Ajay talking about a crore. Hell, they didn't know what a crore looked like!

But Ajay was serious, that much they could tell. 'Yes, a crore,' he said, getting up and walking to the window. 'And I know exactly where to get it. I even know how we can get it. But it'll need a lot of heads, at least twenty people to make it work. How the hell do we get so many men?' He turned back to the others. 'You know what it means, don't you?

More men means a greater risk; one of them may talk, and then we're finished.'

They were all silent. Joginder pulled a face, lost in thought. Sharmaji, who'd perked up enormously when Ajay had dangled the word 'crore' in front of them, picked his nose gloomily. Iqbal too looked blank.

'I don't know how, Ajay,' he said, sighing. 'It's not like we can place an ad in the paper for something like this.'

A second later, Ajay spun around, his eyes gleaming, a wicked smile on his lips. 'Why not?'

'How did all the interviews go?' said Sharmaji, huddled in his armchair. Ajay had just walked into the room they had booked at the Holiday Inn near Andheri.

Ajay nodded as he stretched out on the bed, still fully dressed except for his shoes, which he'd kicked into a corner. 'Went well. I've sized up a few fellows, told them to come tomorrow.'

The three of them – Ajay, Sharmaji and Iqbal – had been interviewing people who'd turned up in response to the ad in the newspapers.

Joginder, meanwhile, had been sent to the target site, to case the joint, as it were. All of them were staying at the hotel – they'd checked in on Wednesday, the day before the interviews – but the meeting point was Ajay's room. From the minute they arrived, they had been impressed by how Ajay seemed to have everything and everyone in control – the hotel waiters, bellboys, porters, everyone seemed to want to wait on them. How, they asked him, but he just winked mysteriously. Clearly, his charm had worked wonders.

There was a coded knock on the door, and Iqbal entered. Ajay sat up. 'Well?' he said.

'Most of them looked pretty innocent. A couple of guys, I don't know. I lost them in the crowd.' He flopped down in a chair next to Sharmaji, grabbed the bottle of whisky on the table and poured himself a stiff one. 'Seemed all right to me.'

He drained his glass in a single gulp, poured himself another tall one and sloshed it down immediately. Sharmaji looked at him critically. 'After that display, I can't believe it all went well.'

'Yeah?' said Iqbal nastily. 'Well, you just sit in a room that's being filled one guy after another, with a total of fifty stinking guys for a whole goddamn day, and you tell me how things are.'

'I just did!' exclaimed Sharmaji indignantly.

Ajay held up his hand. 'Peace. Iqbal, you did a brilliant job. What about Joginder?'

'He's casing the place now. It's like he's lived there all his life! He really blends into that place.'

Ajay nodded. 'Good. He'll get the info we need.' He bent down to the briefcase he'd been carrying with him, and opened it. 'I need to show you something.'

The others watched curiously as he rummaged inside the briefcase, pushing aside clothes and papers. Then finally, with a flourish, he drew out a holster. It was empty.

'Really, Ajay?' said Iqbal, sarcasm dripping from his voice. 'An empty holster? Wow, that shit will scare even the army away.'

Ajay nodded. 'Good, then it worked.' He bent to take off his socks.

'What worked?' said Sharmaji.

When Ajay straightened up, he was holding a gun. A pistol, to be precise.

Sharmaji and Iqbal went rigid with shock. The pistol was pointing right at them.

Then Ajay smiled his mischievous smile. 'I'm not going to shoot you, you idiots!' he said, putting it down on the table.

Sharmaji found his voice. 'Ajay! You?' he cried in disbelief. ' I can't believe this. You're the one who said he would never use an actual weapon.'

Iqbal joined in. 'Yeah, man. What the hell is this? Where did you get it?'

Ajay sat back down on the bed. 'Sit down, please. There's no need to worry.'

Iqbal sat down, still wary. But Sharmaji stood where he was, a thousand apprehensions and fears flitting across his face.

'Please, Sharmaji,' said Ajay kindly. 'Please sit down. You trust me, don't you?'

Sharmaji didn't say anything, and after a moment, sat stiffly on the bed next to Ajay's.

'I know this goes against the way we've been doing things. But you have to trust me. This is too big a job. We may need the firepower. But,' and here, Ajay leaned forward, and spoke as earnestly as he could, 'I won't let anything go wrong. You know me.

I'll plan ahead so we don't have to use this. You have to trust me.'

With great reluctance, Iqbal nodded. But Sharmaji still said nothing, just sat there looking miserable and unsure. Finally, he nodded. 'But,' he said, 'only because it's you, Ajay.'

Ajay inclined his head. 'I won't let you down, I promise.'

Their eyes met, and a look of mutual understanding passed between them.

Ajay got up, carefully put the gun into the holster, and stashed it under his mattress. 'There, forget about it. Now where the hell is Joginder?'

Sharmaji got up, went to the wardrobe and took out his jersey. 'He'll be back soon, don't fret,' he said, his nonchalance sounding very forced. 'Meanwhile, I'm going out for a walk.'

Ajay looked up quickly, searched his face for a moment, then nodded. 'Sure. Take your time, Sharmaji. Be careful,' he said, and went out, to Joginder's room.

From the phone there, he made a call to Priya.

It had been a while since they met. The last time had ended in a fight. He had explained to her that there was one last job he had to do, one last game. And after that, he would give it all up. But she hadn't been happy about it.

Priya answered the phone almost immediately. 'Ajay?'

'Hello, darling. I told you I'd call.'

'I know, I was just afraid you wouldn't.'

'You can forget it now.'

'Did you see the wedding card? Priya weds Badrinath – I wish it was your name.'

'I know, darling, I know, have faith.'

'I will.' She paused, and said, 'Ajay, is this really the last time?'

'I promised you, Priya. I keep my word. This is the last time.'

'Badrinath is an adamant guy. I don't like him much.'

Ajay chuckled. 'Then it's good you won't marry him, isn't it?'

'You'll come for me? Promise?'

Ajay checked his watch. It was time. The packet should have reached her by now. 'Check your verandah,' he told her.

'Huh?'

'Go to your verandah, darling.'

He imagined her putting down the phone and walking out to the verandah, picking up the envelope, then tearing it open to find a flight ticket and a single red rose. She picked up an envelope, which she tore open to reveal a flight ticket and a single red rose.

'I promise, my love,' he said into the phone.

Sharmaji left the room, then went straight down to the lobby and out the door of the hotel. It was pleasantly cool outside. He stood there for nearly a full minute, undisguised, looking around him, deciding which way he would go. Then he abruptly turned and began walking to his left.

It was only when he arrived at the end of the alley that he saw the three men who suddenly accosted him. One of them hit him lightly on the head, from behind, and another shoved a black mask over his head, its eyes and mouth sewn closed. The last thing he saw before he lost consciousness was a gun tucked into the belt of the man in front of him.

Sharmaji had once been a cop. He knew

a police revolver when he saw one and he registered this just before he went blank.

The three men bundled his massive frame into a van, slammed the door shut, and drove away. The whole thing was over in twenty seconds.

Twenty minutes later, Sharmaji opened his eyes. The pain in his head had dulled to a throb. They'd taken off his mask, and his eyes prepared to adjust to the anticipated bright light. But no, it wasn't the room which was brightly lit. In fact, the room was in total darkness. There were two men standing on either side of him, holding flashlights which shone directly into his face. In the glare of that light, he could see nothing beyond. He had no idea where he was.

Suddenly, the darkness in the centre became more solid, and formed into a man. He came forward, put down the chair he was holding in front of Sharmaji, its back facing him, and sat down directly between the lights. His features weren't clear, hidden in semi-darkness, like those of the men who held the powerful flashlights. All he could see about the man in the middle was that he was in his mid-forties, well-built, with close-cropped hair and an almost stereotypical moustache. There was a small scar on his forehead. For a moment, Sharmaji wondered how the man could have managed a scar in the shape of a lightning bolt, then realized it was just a wound that had been stitched up badly.

But the man's eyes were his most fearsome feature. They shone through the darkness, and held Sharmaji petrified in their calm gaze. They were bright and determined, and were full of an energy that seemed to be barely tamed. Right now, they were focused on him.

Then the man spoke. 'Hello, Mr P.K. Sharma. How have you been? My name is Waseem Khan.'

16

The Game Is On

A name. Call me old-fashioned, but I needed a name to put to that babyfaced bastard.

On Tuesday afternoon in Worli, I sat with my able trio of Solanki, Rahul and Ranveer around me and we soon came to the unanimous decision that Sharma's phone needed to be tapped. My informer had told us that Sharma was still in Chandigarh, but if the ad had indeed been put out by his gang, he would *have* to come to Bombay before Thursday. Which left Wednesday.

Which meant that with a whole day remaining, there was a chance that some of the gang might contact him before he left.

And if they did, it would be perfect, because I had just spoken to Singh and got him to bug Sharma's phone.

Singh was not even sure how wire tapping was set up. He kept asking if it happened the way we had watched it in that movie *Inkar*, where Vinod Khanna played a cop and tapped a phone to trace the kidnapper, Amjad Khan. I assured him that we had made lot of technological advances in the last decade.

I could see the scenario playing out as it always had, though: the cop going to Sharma's place, pretending to fix the telephone line because of a complaint he'd received. It was routine stuff, and shouldn't excite suspicion at all. And presumably it hadn't, because a call came through in less than two minutes. Bombay and Chandigarh were both listening in on the conversation.

'Hello? Singh here. Can you hear me?' He was doing a pretty convincing job.

The police operator to whom the call was made sniggered. 'Yes, I can hear you.'

'Listen to this, sir,' Singh said. There was a scrabbling sound, and a deeper voice said, 'This is P.K. Sharma. What's wrong with my phone?'

The operator was clearly expecting this. 'Nothing, sir. Singh has fixed it. Don't worry, the sound is clear now,' he rattled off in a mechanized drone that spoke of utter boredom.

'Okay, okay,' said Sharma, and then Singh was back on the line again. 'Everything all right there?'

'You bloody idiot!' hissed the operator. 'Hang up and get the fuck out of there!'

'Will do, sir,' Singh said and hung up.

All of us listening in heaved a collective sigh of relief. 'Your man certainly has a weird sense of humour,' I said wryly to Singh, who was still listening in from Chandigarh.

'Yeah,' he said apologetically. 'Fellow never learns. He's the best we have, so he does what he wants.'

'Anyway, he's done it. Fingers crossed now,' I said, and hung up.

We hit pay dirt within three hours. The boredom was just settling in when Sharma's phone – and simultaneously, at least another twenty phones in Bombay and Chandigarh – rang. Instantly, there was a mad scramble to find headphones to listen in on, and I pictured the same happening elsewhere too. Well, at least we were closer to where the action would be. Probably.

'Hello?'

It was a flat voice, completely undistinguishable from a million others.

Sharma's deep voice answered. 'Yeah, Ajay, what news?'

Beside me, Rahul started scribbling frantically.

'Did you get the ticket?' the first voice said. It was impossible to place his accent, and I was sure the others were also finding it as hard to put a face to that voice. Could it be the same man in the photographs? Mr X?

'Yeah, I've got the ticket. Spoken to Joginder or Iqbal yet?'

'Yes,' the voice said, and with that, I made up my mind. This had to be the leader. There was too much authority in that voice. No wonder Sharma followed him.

'The two of them will meet you at Delhi airport,' the voice continued.

'What's the matter, Ajay? You sound tense.' Sharma's voice had an unexpectedly kind ring to it.

The other man sighed. 'Nothing, Sharmaji. Just a little tired, I guess.'

'Hey, Ajay, you listen to me. You of all people can't get tired. Let's finish this last one, and then you can be as tired as you want!'

The voice on the line chuckled. 'Don't worry. I'll meet you at the airport tomorrow evening.'

'All right. You take care, okay? Good night,' Sharma said, his voice full of concern.

There was a slight pause. 'I will, Sharmaji, thanks. Good night.' Then he hung up.

Well, well, well. So this was the famous Mr X. Finally, I have a name for you. Ajay. Mr X is Ajay.

As the room burst into activity, Rahul directing most of the officers, I thought about the other thing that had interested me during the conversation. Sharma was clearly quite concerned about Ajay. That meant more than just a professional relationship; Sharma actually cared about this Ajay character. We could definitely use that to our advantage.

Ranveer looked at me, but his face held dismay. He'd noticed the caring tones of Sharma too. 'Sir,' he said, 'this fellow will be hard to crack. He won't give up the gang.'

I patted Ranveer on his shoulder. The kid had a lot to learn. 'You're wrong. He cares for

Ajay, that means he's emotional, which again means he is a softer man than he shows. We can use that. If he doesn't give up the gang because he cares for Ajay, he'll definitely give it up for his family.'

I paused to let the words sink in. Finally, before Ranveer could react, I said, 'But it won't come to that. He'll break sooner.'

Rahul came up and shoved the notepad in my face. The words 'Ajay', 'Joginder', 'Iqbal', 'tomorrow evening', 'last' and 'airport?' were written on it and circled in red. 'The call was from a hotel in Andheri, sir,' he said, and turned to another fellow who sat waiting, headphones on and an expression of self-importance on his face.

'Where was the call made from?'

The man consulted a read-out in front of him. 'The number is 435276. Holiday Inn.'

At last! We had him. 'Which room?' I shouted.

'One moment, sir, I'm just checking...' He turned a few pages and then exclaimed triumphantly, 'Room 1453!'

Good. Time for action. I motioned to Rahul and Ranveer. 'Rahul, get a shadow on Sharma. I want his every movement traced, from his house to the airport to Bombay. He doesn't get to take a leak without us knowing. Ranveer, get Solanki to send out a couple of shadows on Ajay too. Then get me all details you can on him. Nobody makes a move without my orders. I want these fellows caught only when they've got their dirty hands in the jar.'

They scattered. We were ready, a step ahead of the gang, and we just had to stay that way.

I knew exactly how the game would play out the next day. There would be at least three people in Chandigarh, shadowing Sharma and the two others. They would keep switching, so that the targets would never see the same man behind them. One man would follow Sharma from his house, on the interstate bus to Delhi, till the airport, where there would be another shadow waiting. He would then tail Sharma till he met the others and joined the queue for the flight. Finally, another one would follow them into the plane, and then to Bombay.

Here in Bombay, things were falling into place. Within fifteen minutes of finding out where Ajay was holed up, a couple of shadows had landed up there. One of them had gone into the hotel, made surreptitious enquiries as only the police can, and called the control room from a local STD booth. I picked up.

'Sir, he's checked in as S.K. Vardhan. Been at the hotel for a couple of days. Gave a Trivandrum address in the register, it's fake, I checked.'

'Good, keep me posted.'

I turned to Solanki. 'I want to get as close to that hotel as possible. Can you arrange it?'

He thought for all of five seconds before he nodded.

In no time at all, the makeshift PCR was unmade and shifted to a building a stone's throw away from the hotel. We commandeered a room that gave us a direct view of the hotel's front gate. Now, there was nothing else to be done but wait and see what the foursome would attempt.

What the hell had that ad been all about? That was something I couldn't figure out. Why would they need fifty men, exactly how big was this job they were planning? And why the fuck would you advertise in a newspaper? That would be shooting yourself in the foot, if the cops were on to you. I lay awake the entire night with these questions rattling around in my head.

The shadows tailing Ajay called early next morning. Too early. Every single one of us in the new makeshift PCR had fallen asleep out of sheer exhaustion, and the phone jerked more than one of us out of our slumber.

I checked the watch. Seven o'clock. I picked up the phone and barked a hello into it.

'He went to the Jari Mari area, sir—'

'What's that?'

'The place is notorious for forgeries. They make all kinds of forged documents from graduation certificates to American passports.'

'Oh!'

'Yes, sir. It was very crowded, and I don't know if he knew he was being followed, but we lost him for around fifteen minutes before we picked him up again. He didn't seem to be carrying anything, but I'll bet my life he got something done there.'

I could easily take a guess what he'd got there. Badges or CBI shields for his gang, no doubt.

'Where is he now?' I asked, stifling a yawn.

'Back at the hotel.'

'Okay. Keep me posted.'

I hung up and dialled Chandigarh. I knew Singh would be asleep, and it gave me a sneaky sense of pleasure to wake him up.

As it turned out, he was already up. 'Sharma is on the move. Our men are on to him.'

The game was on.

The shadow at Holiday Inn called at four. 'He's on the move, sir. Looks like he's heading for the airport.'

I looked at Solanki, who was also listening in. He nodded. 'We've got men there.'

Nearly two hours later, we saw a hotel car pull up outside, and four men got out. I'd seen two of them before, but this was the first time I was looking at all of them together. They were all there, all four of them. It would be so easy to go over there now. End this all right here, *right now*! But no, it couldn't be done. They would have to be caught in the act.

We watched as the bellboys and porters fell over themselves, following the four men into the hotel. Ajay had them all eating out of his hand, I had to give him that.

Within ten minutes, one of the shadows who'd just come off a shift walked into the PCR. 'They checked into different rooms. Getting royal treatment, the fuckers.'

'All right, all right. Cool it.'

'Sorry, sir. Anyway, they dumped their luggage in their rooms and have regrouped in Ajay's room.'

Solanki gestured at me. 'It's okay, we've got it bugged.'

Moments later, I was glued to the headphones again.

Ajay was talking. '...ordered this just a minute ago.' There was a clink of glasses. 'So, what do you guys think of the ad?'

'I can't believe you actually did that, man!' someone said. We all looked at the shadow. Iqbal, he mouthed.

'This is huge! This is going to be huge!' said another voice, which had to be Joginder's.

Ajay laughed. 'It's the last play after all, guys. It's *got* to be huge.'

Sharma said in his deep voice, 'But fifty men? Why would we need so many?'

'It's a big job, Sharmaji,' said Ajay. 'Besides, I don't yet know exactly how many we'll need. Maybe we won't need all fifty of them.'

'And where's our target?'

Twenty-six pairs of ears perked up. But their owners were soon disappointed. Ajay didn't say anything, but a few seconds later the room erupted in whoops and cheers. There was the sound of a chair overturning, a glass breaking, and then loud laughter.

Iqbal's voice came through. 'Come on, I want to show you guys something. It's in my room.'

I looked quickly at Solanki, who stared back at me in horror. Clearly, they hadn't bugged that room.

There was the sound of a door closing.

I took off my headphones and looked around the room. 'Did anyone hear anything? Anything at all? Where's their target?'

Everyone was silent. Damn!

'He must have showed them a photo or something,' said Ranveer.

I saw Rahul shoot him a dirty look. 'No kidding,' he said.

Ranveer turned to me. 'Sir, why don't we bring Sharma in? Let me have a few rounds with him. I promise he'll sing for you.'

I shook my head. 'No, that's not an option now. Listen,' I said, seeing the look on his face. 'I know you're itching to have a go at him for screwing you like he did. And you'll get your turn, don't worry. But not now. We've got to pull our punches, wait for the knockout blow.'

Ranveer kept quiet, sulking. But I had more important things to worry about. This was bad. They were going to hold that damn interview tomorrow, and we had no idea what they were planning. Or how, or where. We needed to know. And to do that, I could see only one way.

I turned to Solanki. 'I want ten or twelve of your best men. They're going to answer that ad. Maybe Ajay will pick at least one of them. Whatever it is, I want eyes and ears inside there.'

Solanki nodded and left the room.

Well, at least this way we might get lucky. These fellows were being careful, really careful. So we had to be less so, play it a little risky. That was the only way to get results.

We kept up our vigil, but the gang didn't leave the hotel that entire evening. Neither did they return to Ajay's room. Presumably they were in Iqbal's, so we were blind and deaf for the night.

17

The Countdown Begins: Thursday

All the twelve men Solanki had brought with him were assembled in front of me. It was 9.45 a.m., and their interview was about to begin. I looked them over, and they did seem to be the best men Solanki had.

'Keep your eyes and ears open,' I told them. 'Observe everything. Read the man who interviews you. Read his weaknesses and play to them. You've got brains, use them. I don't care what you have to do. Get yourselves into their plan without raising any suspicions. Got it?'

They nodded.

'Good. Now get in there.'

That had been over five hours ago. Whatever the gang was doing, they were certainly running one long marathon of an interview. They were holding it in the hotel's conference room, which we hadn't known, so the room wasn't bugged. In any case, I felt confident that at least six or seven of Solanki's men would be chosen. They were, after all, the best.

I was proven wrong. Rahul, who was watching the whole thing from close quarters, from the lobby, called me on the hotel phone. 'Sir, they're all waiting outside the conference room. The gang is deliberating. It all looks very important. In fact, if I didn't know the truth, I would have been taken in too.'

'The hotel staff certainly believes them,' I grumbled.

'Wait a minute. One of them has come out, he's waving a paper. Hold on.'

I waited patiently, then he spoke again. 'Sir, they've declared twenty-six names. We've got only More and Gupta in.'

'Fine. Stay there a little while longer and then come back in,' I said and hung up.

Just two of them. If we'd got more people in, we could have had more leverage, but just the two of them wouldn't be able to do much, maybe just observe and report.

Solanki was puzzled too. 'Dinesh – he's the really brilliant one. Why wouldn't they pick him?'

'I have no idea, Solanki. We'll know soon enough.'

In another hour and a half, just as the clock struck seven, the twelve men returned one by one. I waited till they were all in, and then asked for a debriefing. What they told me left me even more confused.

'Sir, it was strangest interview I gave.'

'...hardly asked anything of consequence!'

'...they asked me what my favourite song is. What the hell?'

'...only wanted to know if I could speak English...'

'...asked me to show them my biceps, just because I work out.'

'...I mean, how does it matter what my favourite song is?'

'...almost everyone selected is non-Maharashtrian...'

'...I knew I impressed the guy with my answers...'

'...singing songs can't save lives...'

I turned to More and Gupta, who were standing at the end of the line. 'Well?' I said.

'It *was* strange,' said More thoughtfully. 'Their questions seemed standard stuff anyone would ask. Knowing their background, and this Ajay's intelligence, I would have expected more.'

'And anyway,' Rahul interjected, 'if they want more members for the gang, why would they advertise for the CBI?'

'What happened after you two were selected?' I asked.

This time Gupta spoke. 'They got us all back into the conference room. The leader – called himself S.K. Vardhan – gave a pep talk. It was pretty good,' he said grudgingly. 'The man does know how to lead. He got everyone completely worked up. All about working for God and country and shit. By the end, they would've taken a bullet for him.'

More took over, speaking in his brusque manner. 'Told us to report tomorrow at eleven. Said Sharma and Iqbal would take a two-hour class. Apparently, after lunch there'll be a practical exam. That's what they called it. Said they had to see how we would respond in a situation of extreme pressure.'

'Guy's a real linguist, too,' Gupta said. 'Spoke to the Gujjus in Gujarati, the Tamilians in Tamil, to More here in Marathi.'

'Bastard told me not to slouch,' muttered More, clearly disgruntled at being told off. 'You know, he had a name for us. Called us "Special 26".'

Weird. He'd even got a name for them. Not the most imaginative one, clearly.

I looked around at their faces. 'And that's it? Where the hell is the raid?'

More and Gupta looked sheepish. 'He didn't say anything about that.'

So, it hadn't worked. We'd got our men in, but we still didn't know where the raid would be. And it would be tomorrow afternoon, which meant we had less than eighteen hours to figure out where it would be.

There was only one thing left to do.

I turned to Ranveer. 'Looks like we're going with your idea after all, kid.'

I planned it all out, down to the last meticulous detail. It would be tricky, but if handled correctly, without hesitation, without anybody panicking, we could pull it off.

Then, seconds before Operation Bodysnatch could be put into action, our target made it completely irrelevant. One of the shadows on watch called. 'Sharma has just exited the building.'

I looked out of the window, and saw him standing just outside the hotel gate. What the hell was he doing, just standing there? But before any of us could react, he turned and walked to his left.

Well, I could hardly lose such an opportunity, could I? If the man wanted to speak with us so badly, I was the last person to disappoint him.

I turned to Ranveer, who was to have been the lead man in Operation Bodysnatch. 'Looks like we're aborting the beginning and middle of the op and going straight to the end,' I told him, smiling. 'Go bring Sharma in.'

18

Countdown: Thursday Evening

Sharmaji heard the man's voice through the darkness in the room and the blackness of his fear. He knew he had heard the voice before, but his panic-stricken brain refused to let the memory through.

'Remember me, Mr Sharma?" the man said again. 'We met briefly inside a Ludhiana toilet, before your boss bailed you out.'

Finally, Sharmaji's brain allowed the memory to come through, and he drew in his breath sharply.

The man nodded. 'I see you remember now. My name is Waseem Khan.'

Sharmaji's lips moved, but his voice was yet to return.

The man waggled his eyebrows. 'So, Mr Sharma! Looks like you love playing cops and robbers!'

Sharmaji's voice was back, but the words were still locked inside his head. 'N-n-n-no, ugh-ugh-ugh—'

Waseem waved at him to shut up, and Sharmaji did so gratefully.

'Listen to me very carefully, Mr Sharma,' Waseem said, speaking softly, his voice hissing with menace. 'I will ask you some questions, and you will have two choices. The first one is to say you don't know anything.'

He leaned forward. His eyes held Sharmaji in its terror-inducing grip. Then he spoke, and his voice was even colder than before. 'Let me tell you, Sharmaji, for your best interests, choosing this first option would be inadvisable. We can do things to you that nobody even knows can be done. And we will do it with perfect precision. We will take you to the edge of pain and madness and death, but then bring you back, just enough to let you recover, and then begin all over again.

You won't be allowed to die, but you'll wish for nothing else. I promise you that.'

Sharmaji stared at him in horror. There was no doubt in his mind that Waseem meant every single word.

Waseem leaned back. His voice changed, was warmer, kinder. 'The second option is for you to cooperate with us, save us some time and trouble. I can guarantee there'll be no pain involved with this route. In fact, you may even get some relief.'

Sharmaji nodded vigorously.

'Good. Now, where—'

Sharmaji found his voice abruptly. 'Opera House! Jewellery stores!' he cried.

Waseem looked at him questioningly.

Sharmaji hung his head. 'Sorry. I meant the raid will be at Opera House.'

Waseem leaned forward again. 'When?'

'At three p.m.'

'What's Special 26?'

Sharmaji was astounded. How could they know so much? They'd only decided on the name last night!

'It's a big place, sir. We needed more men for... you know.'

'So you placed an ad in the paper? Bold move, Sharmaji. All right, come on. It's a big game, help us out. What's the plan?'

'They'll be given training tomorrow—'

'What kind of training?'

'I mean, just explaining their roles to them. What they would have to do, how to behave, that sort of thing, get them ready.'

'Then?'

'Then?' said Sharmaji miserably. 'Then the bus will come to the hotel at two thirty p.m. sharp. We'll go to Opera House and raid all the jewellers there. Pretend to be CBI, let the Special 26 we recruited help us with it.'

His voice became smaller and smaller. Waseem understood that realization had dawned on Sharmaji – it was all over. The only thing he could do was to cooperate.

'We would have been there for not more than half an hour. The plan was for the four of us to escape with the booty, leave the Special 26 there at Opera House. By the time anyone suspected something was wrong, we would have vanished. In half an hour, we would have taken over eighty lakh rupees...' his voice trailed off.

Waseem changed his line of questioning. 'What's with this Ajay character? What's his background?'

Sharmaji looked around wearily. In half an hour, he seemed to have aged decades. 'Ajay wanted to join the CBI,' he rasped. 'But he didn't cut it, failed the exam. Guess it pissed him off.'

Waseem whistled. 'So he decided to open his own CBI?' he said incredulously.

Sharmaji stayed silent, staring at the floor.

'Tell me something, Mr Sharma,' Waseem said, and something in his voice made Sharmaji look up. 'Do you want to go down with these friends of yours? I can tell you that at your age, spending the rest of your life in jail really wouldn't be a good proposition. Or would you like to save your own hide?'

If there was the slightest ray of hope in those words, Sharmaji scrambled towards it. 'Sir,' he said, tears welling up in his eyes, 'if-if there w-w-was some way, any w-w-way... my kids—'

Waseem interrupted. 'You should have thought of that earlier,' he said, his voice cold again.

Sharmaji looked into those pitiless eyes,

his face a tortured wreck as he tried to form words.

'Come on. I don't have all day,' snapped Waseem.

Sharmaji's body sagged, his head fell forward, eyes closed. 'What do I have to do?' he whispered.

Waseem nodded to his men. One of them turned off his torch, and walked away. There was the sound of a switch being flicked on, and lights flooded the room. The other man turned off his flashlight. But Sharmaji's eyes were still closed.

'For now, do nothing,' said Waseem. 'Forget about our little... chat. Let everything play out the way you've planned. To show you that I'm trusting you, I'm even going to tell you that we have our officers among your Special 26. So don't try to get clever on me. It won't work.'

Sharmaji stayed as he was, just nodded his head.

'I just want to arrest your men,' Waseem said softly. 'I don't want to kill any of you. So don't make me.'

Now Sharmaji opened his eyes and looked up. And got another shock.

They were in his room. In room 1451 of the Holiday Inn. That's where he'd been interrogated.

Staring at him were Waseem's men. And one of them was Ranveer. Recognition dawned on Sharmaji's face.

Waseem noticed the look on his face and laughed. 'Like I said. Don't get clever on me.' He stood up. 'So tell me,' he said, almost conversationally, 'how many of these *raids*...' he paused to underline the sarcasm in the word, 'have you guys held?'

Sharmaji shook his head, looking flustered. In the familiar environment, some of his fear had vanished. But there was no way out. 'We would have hit a half century tomorrow,' he whispered.

Waseem burst out laughing. Unlike Sharmaji, he seemed to have shed years off his frame. 'Well, I have to hand it to you. Just the four of you fellows have created enough trouble for more than a lifetime!' he said, chuckling.

Now Sharmaji seemed offended. 'Yeah?' he sneered. 'Well, it wasn't just the four of us. People like *him* helped too!' He nodded at Ranveer.

A strange look passed over Ranveer's face, and his fists clenched. Looking directly at Sharmaji, he said through gritted teeth, 'Sir, can I have just two minutes with him alone?'

Waseem walked to him and laid his hand on his arm. 'Kid, you'll get all day with him tomorrow.'

Ranveer slowly raised his hand, and flexed his thumb and index finger into the shape of a gun. He pointed it at Sharmaji, pulled an imaginary trigger and had the satisfaction of watching Sharmaji flinch. 'Talk to you tomorrow, pal.'

Waseem walked over to Sharmaji. Very deliberately, he stood with his holster visible, then flicked its button open, looking straight at Sharmaji, who paled. 'One more time, Mr Sharma. Don't try to be clever, and I won't have to do anything I don't want to.'

Suddenly, Sharmaji started to laugh. It wasn't that he was finding anything funny; his relief at surviving the encounter had caused him to lose control. He was laughing hysterically, tears streaming down his cheeks.

'What's the matter?' asked Waseem, unfazed. The others were surprised, but he had seen this kind of reaction countless times.

'Sorry, but I suddenly thought of something Ajju said. He said the man who could catch him hadn't been born yet.'

Waseem shook his head. 'Overconfidence has cost many a genius dear, Sharma. What stuff is your Ajju made of?'

Sharmaji was now laughing uncontrollably. Waseem motioned to the others and they got up and went to the door. Waseem came forward, paused for a second, then slapped Sharmaji hard.

That brought him back to his senses. Wiping away his tears, he looked at Waseem, and felt that chill in his bones again.

'Forget about Ajay and think of yourself,' Waseem told him. 'You've got a lot of work to do tomorrow.'

He spun on his heel, went to the door and walked out, slamming it shut behind him.

A little later, Sharmaji knocked on Ajay's door. 'Ajju, we need to talk. Can you come to my room?'

Ajay nodded. He closed the door behind

him and followed Sharmaji to his room. They went inside, and he saw Iqbal and Joginder were already there. They were fiddling with some papers. 'What's the matter?' he asked.

Sharmaji had had the last hour to think about what Waseem had told him. He knew he couldn't give up Ajay without a reason, and he needed a reason.

Now, he spun around and turned on Ajay. 'You tell us what the matter is, Ajay!' he shouted.

Ajay's eyes narrowed. 'I don't understand.'

'You're using us. I know that. You're just using us!'

Ajay stood still, not moving. ''I'm afraid I still don't understand. I've never used—'

'Oh yeah?' bellowed Sharmaji. 'You get the lion's share of the spoils. Sometimes thirty, sometimes forty, sometimes fifty per cent. We have to divide the rest among us.'

Ajay relaxed a bit. 'Is that what this is about? More money?'

'No. It's about trust. And we don't understand what you're doing with your share.'

Ajay's voice hardened. 'With respect, Sharmaji, what I do with my share is not your business. You have no right to ask me that. Just like I don't ask what you do with yours.'

Sharmaji slammed his hand down on the table. 'Then tell me why you live like you do!'

Now Ajay looked surprised. 'What do you mean?'

'You live in a run-down flat in Dongri. You obviously have enough money to stay at this hotel, and to hire its services. So where does it all go?'

Ajay looked at the other two. 'Do you feel the same way?'

With great reluctance, they nodded miserably. 'It's just that, Ajju, we have no idea who you meet, what you do,' Iqbal said earnestly. 'All that money you get... we would like to know where it all goes. Because you clearly don't spend it on your flat. You don't even have a good car, just a Fiat, and you've sold that too.' He looked around at the others. 'We just want to know if we're being taken for a ride.'

Ajay stared at them silently for a while,

and then walked slowly to the window. From there, he spoke in a low voice, not looking at them. 'None of you know how I grew up. I watched my father die, watched everyone else around me scrabbling for food and what little money they could get. We lived like animals. I loved books, but nobody in our area could afford even a pencil, let along books. My father tried his best, and then when he died, I worked hard and bought the books and pencils and pens and copies. I studied hard and it paid off and I went to high school and college. Somewhere along the way, I realized my story wasn't unique. Across India, people who deserve a lot more – clean homes, good water, medicines, education – were getting nothing.'

He sat down on a chair, still refusing to look at the others.

'The politicians, they're supposed to help. Their job is to protect the weak, help the innocent, be just and kind. But they're the opposite, in every sense. The bastards only think of themselves, how they can grow fat on money that's not theirs and food that's grown by us, live in homes made by us, drive on roads laid by us, wear clothes stitched by us. They depend on us, the common man, for everything. And yet, it is these very people that they trample.'

Ajay's voice hardened again. 'I decided not to depend on them any more. They don't stand for anything except corruption and injustice. So I took the law into my hands. I've been stealing from the rich and corrupt. I've been amassing the money, but it's not with me.'

He looked at the others. 'I have a small trust. I put all the money in it. With it, I've built three schools in West Bengal, Orissa and Bihar. I've also built a hospital in Bankura, in West Bengal, where medicines are free. I'm trying to help the poor, those who actually help sustain our country. The bastards failed me in every test because I refused to give a bribe, because I believed in something good. So I'm trying my best to bloody well take out and break as many corrupt politicians and crooked cops I can find. If their numbers fall, maybe, just *maybe*, we might become a strong country.'

The others were left dumbfounded. Never in a million years could Iqbal have imagined that this was what Ajay was doing with his money; the same loot they used to buy luxuries for themselves, Ajay was using to help others. Joginder stood open-mouthed, flabbergasted that someone who could have become a billionaire many times over from their acquired loot had chosen to be a philanthropist instead.

Sharmaji came forward, utterly shamefaced, and knelt in front of Ajay. 'Forgive me, Ajju. It was wrong of me to say all that.'

Ajay shook his head. 'No, Sharmaji, it wasn't. Maybe I should have told you myself, but to be honest, I didn't know how you guys would take it.'

Sharmaji slapped him reproachfully on the knee. Iqbal and Joginder walked up to him, and clapped Ajay on his back. 'I'll tell you one thing, Ajay,' Sharmaji said, 'the CBI, police, whoever the fuck else rejected you were morons. You're a bigger patriot than them anyway, all of them put together. And you're doing a better job than they are.'

The others nodded.

Ajay smiled at them. The crisis was over.

They all stood up, grinned at each other, and unanimously elected to have a drink. But nobody noticed that Sharmaji's glass was the fullest, and was being drained the most quickly. Several times, he opened his mouth to say something, but changed his mind at the last minute.

He had been looking for a reason to hand Ajay to the cops. But right now, he was left wondering if that would be a good idea at all. Then he thought of his kids, his wife, his family, and hardened himself. Some necessary choices had to be made. No one had said this would be easy.

19

Countdown: Thursday Night

Sharma's interrogation had gone well, better than I'd hoped, to be honest. As I shut the door behind me, I knew he would play on my side. I'd seen enough cowards to know they always batted for whichever they believed was the stronger side.

The three of us reached the lobby of the hotel, and strode to the door. But there was something else I needed to do, something I couldn't hold back much longer. I spoke in a low voice to Ranveer and Rahul. 'Brief More and Gupta one more time. I'll meet you guys tomorrow. Goodnight.'

They said goodnight and walked out of the door.

The lobby was empty except for the receptionist. So I directed my urgent query to him. 'Oi! Where's the toilet?'

Frowning with distaste at this obvious display of uncouthness, the man gestured with a thin hand to the end of the lobby. I nodded my thanks, and walked quickly to the washroom.

As I opened the door, I bumped into another man who was coming out.

'Sorry,' we both said in unison. He stood aside to let me in, and walked out.

It was not until my bladder had emptied itself that the nagging thought took shape. The man I'd just bumped into. Ajay!

I darted out of the door and stood there, looking around. He was nowhere to be seen. I went to the reception again, prepared to kick his ass, and had just opened my mouth when I saw him inside the bar, sitting at the counter with a drink.

What the hell? We'd crossed each other, but he'd shown no sign of recognition, even though he'd seen me inside the toilet in Ludhiana. He'd heard my voice too, but just now, when we spoke, he didn't seem to know me.

Well, that was lucky. But, my cynical self told me, pure luck is rare. I had even caught a glimpse of Ajay inside the train before Sharma had waved goodbye at me. Our eyes had met. There was no way he couldn't have known who I was.

But then, that meant—

A nasty, stupid idea formed in my head. My common sense screamed at me to ignore it and walk out NOW, because if I was wrong, it would blow the whole mission. But then…

I went to the bar and pushed the door open. Going right up to the counter, I sat down, leaving a couple of seats between Ajay and me, and asked for the menu.

Now that I was committed to the rash move, my heart slowed to its regular rate, and my eyes and brain took over, absorbing all the details around me, especially those around Ajay.

He was a nondescript chap, up close. There was nothing, absolutely *nothing* to distinguish him. That's why he managed to evade everyone, I realized. He was just so plain that your eyes slipped over him, refused to register such an everyman. He was wearing a pair of cream trousers, and a green shirt which flared at the collar. His eyes were intent upon his glass, like a man mulling life's mysteries in his mind. Beside the glass was a wedding card. I could just make out the words 'Priya Weds Badrinath'.

I glanced at the menu. Looking up, I saw the bartender who'd handed me the menu watching me in polite expectation. I jabbed at the menu. 'So much for just one drink? How much is it?'

The man's face was blank. 'Thirty ml. Sir.' The 'sir' came as an afterthought, forced.

'Anything smaller than that?'

'No, *sir*.'

'All right, all right. Get me a beer.'

Bloody hell. Four hundred rupees for a shot of whiskey! This was definitely the costliest risk I'd ever taken on my own tab, fiscally speaking.

The bartender stomped off. I looked over at Ajay, who was still staring at his drink. Time for the hook.

'Hello,' I said, keeping my voice as casual as possible.

He looked up at me. 'Hello,' he said, and smiled.

He knew. And he knew that I knew. And I could tell from the look in his eyes that he wasn't going to stop.

'Hello,' I said again, feeling a little foolish. He nodded.

I stuck out a hand across the empty stools. 'Waseem,' I said.

He looked at me for a microsecond, and took my hand. 'Vardhan,' he said. We shook hands.

'So,' I said, still keeping my voice casual, 'what is it that you do, Mr Vardhan?'

Ajay looked down at his drink again. 'I'm in sales.'

I pointed at the card. 'Your relative? Badrinath?'

He looked at the card as if he'd suddenly become aware of it. Then he took it, folded and stuffed it into his pocket. 'No,' he said. 'Just some unlucky chap.'

The bartender arrived with my drink and put it down in front of me, along with soda and water. I was damned if I was going to pay for that, Ajay or no Ajay in front of me. 'I didn't ask for soda,' I said.

The bartender sighed theatrically. 'Complimentary.' The 'sir' was altogether gone now, I noticed.

'All right, fill 'er up.' He did, and left.

I took a swig, looked up and saw Ajay watching me, a strange look on his face. 'What line of work are *you* in?' he said.

'Government service,' I said.

'Really?' he said, apparently perking up. 'Government does service too? Cheers!'

I smiled back. 'Cheers! Why, do you have a quarrel with the government?'

'Quarrels are for the weak, Waseem saab…'

'And people like you?'

He chuckled. 'People like me just enjoy our drinks quietly, live out our lives.'

'What's the verdict?'

He looked at me, shook his head and got up. 'Charge the bill to my room,' he told the bartender, and stuffed some cash into his hand as a tip. Then he looked at me. 'Goodnight, Waseem saab.'

I nodded. 'Goodnight.'

Cool motherfucker! I wondered, what he would do if I…

Swiftly, I brought out my wallet, took out a hundred-rupee note, and dropped it to the floor. 'Mr Vardhan,' I shouted.

Ajay turned, and watched as I picked up the money. 'You dropped this.'

He came closer, and I handed him the note. 'It's yours, isn't it?' I asked.

He nodded. 'Yes, yes, of course. Thank you.' Then he turned and strolled out.

Arrogant, greedy bastard. Wouldn't even let go of a hundred bucks!

All right, Ajay. You'll pay for that. I'll take you out personally.

20

Setting It Up

Holiday Inn, Friday, 11 a.m.

D-Day dawned, bright and sunny. It was a good day to get rich or get caught, thought Ajay, as he waited in the conference room with Iqbal and Joginder. Sharmaji, uncharacteristically, was late. When he finally turned up, he looked drawn, as if he hadn't slept the night.

The clock struck eleven. One by one, the Special 26 poured into the room.

Ajay stepped forward and spread his hands wide. 'This is it,' he said, slowly pacing from one side of the group to the other. 'This is why you're here. This is your ultimate test, to see if you are fit to be part of the most elite agency in the country. You are the Special 26, the smartest, the best and the most intelligent. Don't get scared. Nobody fucks around with us, remember that. If anyone tries, don't let them. Crooks should see you and tremble in their boots.' He stopped in front of Gupta. 'Remember, strength lies in your heart. Never for a fucking moment doubt what your heart tells you.'

Nobody saw Sharmaji shaking his head in disbelief.

'Once the raid is conducted,' Ajay continued, 'you will all come back here. If everything's in order, you will get your appointment letters. Now, Mr Roy here...' he pointed at Sharmaji, 'will give you your orders. Follow them to the letter.'

Sharmaji took over. He was back to his usual self.

'Remember, you're the highest authority here,' he said, glaring at the group. 'No one has the power to stop you. No one can stop you. No one can come between you and your duty. Do you understand?'

There was a chorus of perfectly harmonized 'yes, sir's.

Sharmaji nodded approvingly. 'Good. Now listen carefully.'

Ajay left them to it, and quietly walked out of the room.

Opera House Showroom, Friday, 9 a.m.

At 9 a.m. sharp, I entered the jewellery showroom. It was a swanky affair, glass everywhere, neon lights, fluorescent lights, all designed to reflect as much glitter as possible. Ranveer and Solanki were waiting for me in the lobby. There was another man with them, a fat man with a ring on every finger, at least a couple of bracelets on each wrist, a chain around his neck, enough gold to weigh down the goddamn *Titanic*. And he had a look of anxiety on his face.

Solanki introduced us. 'Sir, this is Magandas Singhania, the owner of this establishment. Maganji, this is Waseem Khan, CBI.'

A look of panic flitted across Magandas's face. 'C-C-CBI? But why?'

I glared at him. 'That's it, Mr Singhania, that's exactly the reaction they take advantage of. Sethji, your establishment will be looted today.' I took a certain malicious pleasure in giving the man a shock.

All I managed to do was to make him look more anxious than before. 'Wh-what do you mean?'

'At about three this afternoon. Around thirty men will turn up posing as CBI officers to loot your shop.' I gave him a look. 'I believe I'm correct in assuming you'd want to avoid being looted like that?'

The man nodded emphatically.

'Good. Do you have a safe place to stash the goods until all this is over?'

'Everything?'

'Yes, everything, everything that's in the shop,' I snapped.

'Oh! I have a factory, everything can be stored there.'

'How far?'

'Not too far, at Andheri MIDC, about an hour from here.'

'Good. We'll replace all your jewellery with our own marked jewellery. So you have to shift everything you have out of here and into that factory. Do it within half an hour.'

Magandas shrieked. 'Half an hour? But how can I do it in half an hour?'

I was not in the mood to tiptoe. 'Look, it's quite possible. Get it done. They're going to clean out your shop in half an hour. I don't want any of your employees here. I'm going to replace them all with my men and the police. You will close your shop for the public. There will be customers in here, but they will be our officers.'

Magandas scratched his head. 'Sir, if you know everything, why don't you just arrest them where they are?'

I snapped. Here we were trying to save his ass, and he was trying to avoid any inconvenience to himself. I grabbed his shirt and pulled him close so that his nose was an inch from mine. At this distance, I could smell the fear on him. 'Listen to me, Sethji. There's no law against thinking up a crime. We can get them only if they commit the crime. And that too, when we have proof that they're guilty. So what's it going to be? Will you handle it on your own, or get the fuck out of the way so I can save your ass?'

The look on Magandas's face was answer enough.

I left Solanki and Ranveer to coordinate with him, then went and dialled Rahul at Holiday Inn. 'What's going on there?'

'It's all good, sir. As expected. The training is going on.'

'Anything we need to be worried about?'

'Nothing, sir.'

'Good. Keep me posted.'

I went back to the lobby. Solanki was there, gazing at a map. He looked up as I approached. 'I've got a map of this area. It should help.'

I motioned to him to follow me. We went up to the terrace, Solanki still clutching the map. I pointed at buildings around us. 'Forget the map,' I said. I hated maps, only used them when absolutely necessary. Far better to get to a high vantage point and look around you. That way, you get the feel of the place. 'I want a sniper here, here and there. There should be no way the bastards can get out alive, all right?'

Solanki nodded and rushed off. Directly in front of me, on the street below, an armoured van had arrived. Magandas's stuff was being loaded into it under the watchful eyes of Ranveer and the anxious eyes of Magandas.

I went down the stairs, taking them two at a time, and came out into the lobby. I went to the van and checked it thoroughly. I turned to Ranveer. 'How much longer?'

He didn't take his eyes off the loading. 'Another five minutes, I guess.'

'Hmm. Once you're done, check the CCTV setup here.'

He nodded. When the loading was done, the van drove off silently, six armed officers inside, and a couple of police cars following it.

I walked to a nearby paan shop. I needed a cigarette. The man saw me approach, but mistook me for a bystander. 'Gimme a Gold Flake,' I barked at him. He was more interested in what was going on behind me, and was staring at the van. 'Hey!' I said. 'Gimme a Gold Flake.'

He was about to retort, something rude no doubt, when Solanki ran up behind me. 'Snipers in place, sir.'

'Good.' I squinted into the distance. 'I need more men. Two plainclothes there, and there. At both ends of the road. I want two more there, where they'll park the bus. And get me another seven–eight men. I want them scattered among these locals.'

'Yes, sir,' said Solanki and rushed off.

I turned to see the paanwallah looking at me round-eyed, a cigarette packet held in his quivering hand. His face was a mask of terror, no doubt because of the sudden appearance of the uniform-clad Solanki and my orders to him.

'I asked for just one.'

The man fumbled with the packet, his normally dexterous fingers tearing at the plastic wrapper. Finally, he extracted a cigarette and handed it reverentially to me. Before I could ask, his hands had cupped a match in front of me, although it took me a good few seconds before I could light the cigarette because of his violently shaking hands. I nodded to him, took out a one-rupee note and left it on the counter.

Holiday Inn, Friday, 2 p.m.

'What's wrong, Sharmaji?' said Ajay, leaning against the desk in the conference room behind which the older man was sitting.

'Wrong? Nothing, why?' said Sharmaji, looking green.

'You seem very tense today,' said Ajay.

Sharmaji smile was sickly. 'I'm growing old, I guess. Can't take the stress any more.'

Ajay laughed. 'Come on! This is our last

time, enjoy it. And anyway, you don't have to worry. I'm leading today, remember?'

Sharmaji nodded. But before he could say anything more, Joginder burst through the door. 'The bus is here.'

Ajay looked at his watch. 2 p.m., bang on time. 'All right, load everyone up.'

He stood up and slung his bag over his shoulder. Then he looked at Sharmaji and smiled. 'Game on.'

Opera House, Friday, 2 p.m.

The phone rang. It was Rahul. 'Sir, the bus has arrived. Nobody in sight yet.'

'Good. Stay on the line. I want real-time reports.' I turned to Solanki and directed a questioning look at him. 'We're fully ready,' he said.

Ranveer came up and nodded. 'CCTV working perfectly, sir.'

Rahul started speaking again. 'Sir, they've made a rush for it. They're all in the bus now!'

'Is Ajay in there?'

'He was standing at the front, so yes, has to be.'

'Okay.'

'Sir, they're taking their seats… the bus is starting… it's moving now… it's at the gate… it's paused at the gate, driver's looking both ways… rolling again… the bus is leaving… sir, the bus has left, repeat, the bus has left!'

Talk about a real-time report.

I hung up and turned to the others in the room. Everyone was standing at attention. 'Okay, listen up! The bus has left the hotel. It'll be here in an hour. Anyone wants to take a leak or something, go do it now. You won't get time later. But remember this. Nobody, and I mean *nobody*, must escape today. I want them alive. If they try to make a run for it, take them down, *shoot* them down if you have to. Nobody gets out of here alive, got it?'

There was vigorous nodding around the room.

'Good. Now, none of you make a move until I say so. Wait for my signal. Do not, repeat, do not move before I signal.'

I pointed to Solanki. 'You'll monitor from the terrace.' He nodded.

I turned to Solanki's number one. 'Shinde, you'll monitor the traffic police. I want eyes at all times on the bus.'

'I've already mobilized the traffic department, sir. And our men are following the bus in unmarked cars.'

'Good. Ranveer, you will be at the edge of the road. Make sure nobody gets out.'

'Yes, sir.'

I looked around one last time. This was it. 'Good luck, guys.'

I went up to the terrace of the building opposite Opera House. From time to time, the radio crackled as the teams following the bus and the traffic police gave us updates on the location of the bus. I looked around. Everything was in place. The street below looked normal, exactly as on any other day.

I was feeling calm too. All was going according to plan. Sharma was working for us, and we knew he hadn't told Ajay about being a double for us.

The bus would be here soon. Any minute now. *I've got you, Ajay.*

21

The Sting

Opera House, Friday, 3 p.m.

The four snipers were in place, armed and ready, nothing would escape them.

So were the men down in the street. And those inside the barber's shop. And those waiting at the bus stop. And the ones near the run-down theatre. Hell, the bootblack was a cop too, and yes, he too was ready.

I stood on the terrace of the four-storey building, my foot resting lightly on the edge as I surveyed my surroundings for the hundredth time.

I looked at the building directly opposite. It looked like a giant mirror and some cement had mated, and the result was one of the most sparkling, immaculate jewellery storerooms in the city, complete with bright lights, tasteful neon sign, brilliantly polished glass windows and doors — even the security guard's belt buckle was a bronze mirror. This was one jeweller who had struck gold, I thought, smirking at my own pun. Well, the jeweller in the shop had some company — there were cops in there with him too. Today they were jewellery connoisseurs.

Down on the street, everything looked exactly as it should. Except that none of it was as it should be. The man at the corner, getting his shoes polished, had too round a bulge in his jacket to be carrying a book. A holster, maybe. Shailesh.

The bootblack polishing the shoe kept an eye on everything around him too. Occasionally, he sneaked a hand inside his kit, and checked on the gun hidden there. Ravi. And across the street, Nair, the coconut man.

I looked at all the officers one by one. The man on the bench reading the paper. The seemingly unemployed duo chatting on the pavement near the signal. The men at the garage repairing some auto parts. And of course, the men sprinkled inside the building opposite and those inside the shop itself. The place was swarming with police. A lone constable paced the area; if he hadn't been present, anyone staking out the site would have been instantly warned away.

Suddenly, I saw a flash of light. The man at the traffic lights had just given me the signal, flashing the sun off his steel-encased watch right in my eyes. Showtime.

As I craned my neck and waited to see what was coming up the road, there was a subtle change in the atmosphere on the street too. People suddenly became preoccupied and hyper-attentive.

Then I saw the bus. It seemed to be full of people who were barely moving as it lumbered slowly along the road, inching closer as the driver navigated the narrow, dingy path. Why the hell wasn't it stopping? Was it the bus we were waiting for?

The next moment, the bus stopped.

This was it. They were all here. It all begins now.

Except that it didn't. Nothing began. The bus just sat there, doing nothing.

Nobody moved in the street. Well, no, everyone was moving, going about their chores, though in their minds they were all standing absolutely still, waiting to see what would happen next. Who would act first?

Nothing happened. The bus was still exactly where it had stopped.

I was too far away, high up on the terrace, and couldn't see what was happening inside the bus. I looked at the sniper on the next roof, and he slowly drew his walkie-talkie out with his left hand, the right hand holding the gun still. My radio crackled. 'No visual. The glass is tinted.'

Shit. Whatever the hell they had been planning, it surely couldn't be this.

I spoke into my radio, broadcasting to all officers. 'Nobody move. Repeat, nobody move.'

I needed a moment. I had to figure out what they were doing before ordering any move. Except that, however furiously I thought, I could come up with no explanation.

My radio crackled. It was Ravi, the bootblack. He was leaning forward, as if he'd dozed off, and hiding the radio under his clothes as he spoke. 'Sir, I can see the driver. He's not moving. Just sitting there.'

Nair broke in, hunched down behind the coconut stall. 'I can take him. I'm nearest the door, I can take it out, get in, neutralize—'

'No, you idiot!' I said through gritted teeth. 'Stand down, repeat stand down.'

'Sir,' Nair continued doggedly. 'It might be a bomb.'

Fuck. He could be right. For a moment, I thought he was. And if it was a bomb, delaying would be the worst thing we could do. If it exploded, it would take out the entire street, and before local cops and fire brigade arrived, the gang could have come, grabbed the loot and fled. Of course, they would get fake stuff, but they would have *escaped*!

I almost panicked. I couldn't let that happen. Not when so many people's lives were at stake.

But then, a thought struck me. Not once, in all the case files I'd read about these guys, had I noticed such violence. True, they had slapped around a few people, but never had they resorted to violence. Hell, I didn't even remember seeing a single mention of a gun being brandished.

Plus, a bomb like that wasn't really the gang's MO. Not if I'd read Sharma correctly, and what he thought of Ajay. No, it couldn't be a bomb.

I spoke into the radio. 'It's not a bomb, repeat, not a bomb. Don't worry about that.'

But it *could* be a thousand other things. And right now, it didn't seem like the bus was going to move. All right. We'd wait half an hour. It had already been five minutes since the bus arrived, so another twenty-five minutes to go. 'We wait for half an hour. Everyone on high alert,' I said.

Half an hour later, there was still no sign of anyone emerging from the bus. This was going nowhere.

Fuck it. Something had to be done.

'Ravi, Nair, you're up. Approach the bus. Exercise extreme caution. Eyes on the driver at all times, watch him for any sudden moves. Snipers, I want all eyes on the bus. Full backup to Ravi and Nair. Respond to any hostile activity with extreme force.'

That's it. We were committed.

Both men slipped their weapons under their clothes, got up and approached the bus casually, as if they were just stretching their legs. I had to hand it to Ravi, especially. He was cool as ice.

Both of them sauntered in the general direction of the bus, and finally, Ravi was in line with the door. He was waiting for my command. I didn't hesitate. 'Move in.'

Swiftly, without a word, Ravi pulled out his gun, yanked open the door and threw himself to one side to avoid any retaliatory fire. 'Police!' he yelled. 'Nobody move!'

Behind him, five more officers had materialized, all with guns aimed at the windows. On the other side of the door, Nair was covering. Shailesh had sprinted across the road and was now covering the driver's door to make sure he didn't make a run for it.

But there was no retaliation. Slowly, Ravi moved in front of the door, and lowered his gun. Then he spoke into the radio. 'I don't get it! These people look scared shitless! Hold up!' He cocked his gun again and aimed at the door. 'There's movement. Someone coming forward... What the hell! It's More!'

What the hell! Why would they just sit there? And why would More and Gupta also be quiet as a mouse in there? This didn't make any sense. Unless...

Oh fuck ! Please no. Please let it not be so…

I ran down the flight of stairs to the makeshift PCR there, and dialled Rahul's number. 'What's going on there?'

Rahul sounded surprised. 'What do you mean? The action is at your end!'

'Anything happening there at all?'

'No, nothing. The bus left, our men followed, that's it! Why?'

I hung up. No no no NO! This couldn't be happening!

I ran down the rest of the way to the street, where one by one, the 'CBI trainees' were filing out, looking scared to death. It was as I'd feared. Ajay and his gang weren't among them.

A bewildered Solanki appeared behind me. 'Sir, what happened?'

It was all coming back to me.

'Well, I have to hand it to you. Just the four of you fellows have created enough trouble for more than a lifetime!'

Sharmaji seemed offended. 'Yeah?' he sneered. 'Well, it wasn't just the four of us. People like him helped too!' He nodded at Ranveer.

Of course.

More flashbacks.

The AD sighed. 'I want to show you something, Khan. Come here.' He got up and went to the window to his right. I went with him.

'See that man there? He's the one those bastards took for a ride.'

I peered through the glass, interested. The man I saw was sitting hunched on a chair, the picture of dejection, twirling his cap nervously in his hands. He was talking to my man Rahul.

The AD went back to his chair and sat down. 'He's a promising kid,' he said.

The AD's words kept echoing back at me. *'That kid went on the hunt, started sniffing around all by himself. He dug up all that dirt on his own.'*

And he'd got me, hook, line and bloody well sinker.

'I know fully what I've done, sir,' he said in a low voice. 'You don't have to insult me for me to know that. I need your help, which is why I came here. If you help me, we can sort this out quickly. But even if you refuse to help me, don't make the mistake of assuming I'm giving up. I won't rest, sir. On my own, it'll take me much,

much longer, but I'll get them in the end, sir. One way or another, I'll get them, I promise you that.'

The mole.

A wan smile was all I could manage. 'Solanki, how many men do we have?'

'You mean, in this operation? Let's see.' He paused as he did a quick headcount.

'We've got twenty-seven men, sir.'

I shook my head. 'You should count again,' I said bitterly. 'Ranveer isn't here. He isn't one of us.'

A great laugh churned inside me. I fought it back down, and turned to him. 'Remember Special 26, Solanki? Ajay's name for the fake recruits?'

Solanki glanced at the scared men now milling around us. Then he looked back at me.

I started laughing. This was completely beyond my control. I shook my head. 'I didn't think Ajay was so unimaginative that this Special 26 was all he could come up with. And he isn't.'

I was laughing hysterically now. Nothing about the situation or the people who were looking at me strangely was funny, but that only made it madder, more hilarious. '*We're* the Special 26, Solanki! WE'RE the bloody idiots he's been playing from the beginning.'

Solanki frowned. 'But then, that means…'

I nodded, tears streaming down my eyes while the others tried to calm me down. 'Yes. Call Magandas's factory. They must have got there by now.'

22

The Hit

MIDC, Andheri, Friday, 3 p.m.

A minibus bearing four stern-looking officers dressed in safari suits and a police car containing several uniformed men (including a lady police officer) halted outside Magandas's factory at MIDC, Andheri. The sight of the vehicles and the officers alighting from them was enough to cause palpable tension in the air.

While the police officers cordoned off the area and began manning the entry and exit points of the jewellery unit, the four officers walked swiftly inside and demanded to see the manager.

A bespectacled man dressed in a starched kurta and dhoti came towards them, hands folded in a namaste. He was trembling like a leaf. These men seemed imposing, and having the police visit a jewellery-making unit spelt trouble with a very big T. 'Sir, I am Shantilal Jain, what is this about?' He was so nervous, he could barely speak.

Sub-inspector Ranveer, who led the police team, told Jain, 'These are CBI officers. They have come directly from Delhi, and have information about malpractices in your unit. We've been told that you are conning people.'

Ranveer looked efficient, and spoke in his most professional tone. The coldness of his voice and his uncompromising demeanour would have rattled anybody. It was said of the Delhi Police that they were experts in terrorizing people, while their Bombay counterparts were good at framing innocents. Ranveer looked every inch the Delhi cop, though no one noticed the anomaly of his uniform, which was that of the Bombay Police.

Interrupting his harangue, Ajay stepped in as if in a reconciliatory manner, 'Enough, officer, let me talk to him.' Dressed in a safari suit and wearing glares, Ajay looked every inch the CBI officer.

He flashed his ID and said, 'We are CBI. We have information that your gold is not pure 24 carat and that you pass off 22 carat gold as 24 carat. We hear that you are fooling unsuspecting customers. We could arrest all of you and put you behind bars for an entire lifetime.'

Jain seemed to have lost his composure. First of all, anything to do with the police terrified him. The word 'prison' made him nauseous. He was pale, yet managed to stutter, 'S-sir, I s-swear by God this is all genuine jewellery.'

Now it was Sharmaji's turn to take over. 'Okay, Mr Jain, we would like to believe that your jewellery is genuine. You have the option of letting us examine the entire lot of jewellery in our CBI unit in Colaba. If we find them to be genuine, we will return the jewellery and withdraw the case.'

Jain heaved a sigh of relief. 'Sir, please do so. Our jewellery has passed the highest scrutiny.'

'Officers, please collect the jewellery in a

bag and make a panchnama and receipt for Mr Jain. Please do it quickly as we have to cover ten more jewellery-making units today,' Ajay told his men.

Iqbal and Joginder began collecting the jewellery even as they made out receipts. The goldsmiths helped them fill in the details.

In less than twenty minutes, the raid was over and the bags, stuffed with jewellery, were placed in the minibus.

The panchnama and receipt were handed over to Jain. There was a CBI stamp on it, signed by Ajay. The officers trooped back into the police van and left the premises, leaving behind them a whole assembly in a state of shock. Everybody in the industrial estate was now talking about the raid at Magandas's unit. If officers from the CBI, from Delhi, had to fly down for this raid, surely the Magandas jewellers were crooks, they conjectured.

Jain was left shell-shocked by the raid. What a day! Never in his fifty years of existence had anything as eventful happened to him. He had never lost his mind the way he had today. All his cognitive abilities had simply deserted him. His heart was still pounding wildly and he was covered in sweat. Was he having a heart attack? But it wasn't the state of his heart that was bothering him. It was that of his personal fortunes. He calculated that the CBI officers had carted away jewellery worth over Rs 1.15 crore.

Jain wondered whether Sethji had any inkling about the raid. Why else had he shifted the jewellery from the showroom to the factory only this morning? Jain had not been very happy. What a burden to bear – and how horribly he had been relieved of it!

Well, now he needed to call Sethji and brief him about the raid. It was not a pleasant task. As he went to the table to dial Singhania's direct line, he saw the phone wires were cut. He was surprised and went to the other phone. Those wires were also neatly clipped. Jain was flummoxed. It crossed his mind that perhaps it was a routine procedure carried out by CBI raiding officers, to cut the phone lines as a precautionary measure.

He was about to proceed to the neighbouring unit, to make a call, when he saw a peon coming towards him. 'Jain sahib, how come both your phones are not working? There is a call from the showroom.'

Jain stumbled as he rushed towards the phone and blurted out in haste, 'Malik, this is Jain.'

Rahul, who had been trying the factory number for a long time, had finally had to call at the neighbour's.

'Jain, why are your phones not working?'

'Sir, those CBI officers had come. They raided our factory and took away all the jewellery for examination. They also cut our lines.'

Rahul turned towards Singhania, who clutched at his chest and collapsed on the nearest chair.

23

Meltdown

Opera House, Friday, 4.30 p.m.

I'd been right. Ranveer was nowhere to be found. His walkie-talkie had been left inside the store. The arrogance of the fucker, he'd even left a note for me with it. It read, 'Sorry, Waseem saab. But I won't need this any more.'

The factory had been raided, just as I'd suspected. Ranveer must have taken some hired help with him; that jewellery-making unit could not have been tackled by four or five men.

That was where I needed to head now. I had to hope that the gang had left behind some kind of trail. Though, of course, I was being optimistic. They had never left anything to sniff after during any of their earlier heists.

Rahul arrived just as the clock struck five. He took one look at me, and I realized that he was concerned. He had good cause. I would have been concerned about myself too, except that right now, I didn't give a damn.

Rahul and I, along with Solanki, got into a jeep and headed towards the factory. Two more jeeps filled with policemen followed us. Nobody spoke.

Through the haze, my subconscious was trying to tell me something, but I wasn't ready. I wasn't willing to listen to it. Not before I'd drowned myself in alcohol and smoke. I was looking out of the window, numbed with failure, when I saw something my brain recognized, but I didn't consciously process the information. Mildly surprised as I was, yes, I let it go.

The traffic was maddening, as has always been the case with any part of central Bombay, no surprise. But things were particularly worse today, with all the wedding cars and—. Wedding! Of course, that's what I had seen a second ago. I asked the driver to stop.

The jeep screeched to a halt, as did the two other jeeps behind us. I got out and started walking back. Rahul ran after me, and caught me by my arm. 'What're you doing, sir?' he said, genuinely concerned.

I couldn't tell him. I had already made enough blunders, and was looking like a fool. I couldn't ask anyone to trust my instincts.

'It's nothing, Rahul. Just a hunch. Listen to me. Get to the factory. Take everyone with you. I'll meet you there.'

He looked unhappy. 'I'll stay, sir. Let the others go on to the factory.'

I laid a comforting hand on his shoulder. 'Thanks, lad. But this I've got to do myself. Even if it's just to convince myself I'm not off my head.'

He gave me a searching look, and went back to the jeep. I heard him barking orders, and in a moment, all three vehicles roared off in the direction of the factory.

The sign had been just around the corner, I told myself as I jogged back. And then I saw it. *Priya Weds Badrinath.* I knew I'd seen it before, in Ajay's hands back at the bar. And

I knew there was no chance he'd be here, not after today's events. So what the hell was I doing here?

Sometimes, fate can crush you completely. But sometimes it lets through a glimmer of hope.

24

Home Run

Santacruz Airport, Friday, 5 p.m.

Sharmaji was laughing his heart out. He was making a hooting noise with a paper napkin. He was back-slapping everybody, generally having a whale of a time. They were in a restaurant and it was celebration time.

Oh, Sharmaji felt so light, like a balloon. It had been nerve-wracking until the job got done. At one point, he had thought that this time the law would finally catch up with them. With the CBI on their tail, it was touch and go. The more he had thought about the heist, the more impossible it had seemed.

But with Ajay, you never lost. How could he have doubted his plan for even a second?

He had planned for them to 'grab' him. He'd thought that at some point, especially if they were frustrated enough, the CBI might target one of them. So, to avoid their picking up Iqbal or Joginder, who would definitely have broken under their intense grilling, he made sure that they picked Sharmaji, who had been a cop and knew all the tricks. And Sharmaji had walked into their trap, safe in the knowledge that they had no idea it was actually a trap for them, set by Ajay. In fact, Sharmaji marvelled at how Ajay had included the stakeout at Opera House as part of the plan. He knew that there would be a description out on him after the goof-up in Calcutta, when they'd walked in on the income-tax raid. And so, he turned it to his advantage. He'd let the cops see him, recognize him. The perfect bait. And in the end, the whole plan had come together like a well-oiled piece of clockwork.

They had all left exactly at the same time as the bus had. Sharmaji had given strict instructions to rush into the bus in an almost chaotic manner, and in the hubbub, the four of them had sneaked out from the rear of the bus, got in the car they'd hired for the day, and headed out to Andheri, to Magandas's factory. On the way they had swapped the car for a minibus. The cops, of course, were none the wiser, and assumed, just as Ajay had said they would, that the four of them had boarded the bus with the new 'recruits'.

At the factory, Joginder and Iqbal played their role well. It was almost as if all the forty-nine times they had raided other homes and godowns and bars and shops had been dry runs, all of it leading up to this one heist. And what a heist it had turned out to be. Magandas had taken Waseem's instructions more seriously than anyone knew. He had transferred not only everything he owned to the factory, but had urged his associates and friends in Opera House to do the same. So, ultimately, the gold, diamonds and silver amounted to over a crore in value.

It was all Iqbal and Joginder could do to not break into a smile during the raid. They confiscated every single thing they could lay their hands on, from the smallest earring to the chunkiest gold chains, glittering in their newness, and diamond pendants shaped like lotuses and hearts. Everything went into the bags the four had brought with them. Just like before, the man in charge of the factory was bullied into submission, and just like before, he signed the official-looking piece of paper without bothering to check its authenticity, and stood there looking broken as he watched the four of them speed away in the minibus.

Unlike before, though, they had Ranveer, and he had brought his own muscle with him, including the lady cop Shantiji and others who had helped them raid the minister's bungalow in Delhi. Taking out an entire factory was quite different from working a shop or even a bungalow, after all. Ranveer was the one in proper uniform, the 'local' police helping the CBI with their raid. And unlike last time, Ranveer and his men and Ajay and the three others left at the same time.

A little ahead, Ranveer's car slowed to a stop, and his hired muscle got out, having earned more than they could have imagined. Their silence, at least, was completely bought. Sharmaji marvelled at Ajay's ingenuity. It had worked, they had been successful. Ajay's plan, which he had been working on for several months, had finally borne fruit. Sipping lassi and tea, they swore they'd never doubted his plan – even though every one of them, Ajay included, had felt, more than once, a sinking feeling of dread and impending defeat.

But here and now, basking in the warm glow of success, all that was in the past. Now, they would head home. And this time, they would all fly. No more trains, Iqbal had said jokingly. It was great for it to not be a joke any more. Meanwhile, Ranveer would stash the loot in a safe place that only he and Ajay knew of. Later, when the heat had cooled, the five of them would meet there again, and finally take away their share. The thought of all that money was uplifting, and it was with light hearts that they looked forward to leaving the city and its cops far behind.

But not Ajay. He wouldn't go immediately, he would part ways with the others and meet up with them later. He had to pick up Priya first. She would be waiting for him. One by one, the others said their goodbyes. When it was Sharmaji's turn, he simply stared at Ajay, a lump in his throat. There were no words to express what he felt, no way to show how much he'd enjoyed every moment of his life ever since the day he'd met Ajay back at the garage. They'd been through a lot since then, and although Sharmaji knew he was not half as smart as Ajay was, he knew that he loved him and was certain that Ajay loved him too. It would be hard to imagine a life without Ajju. They embraced, and Ajay patted him on the back. Pulling back, he said, 'Don't worry, Sharmaji. I'll be around.'

The two of them laughed. Then Ajay got up and held out his hand. Ranveer stood up and shook it. 'It was an honour working with you,' he said.

Ajay shook his head. 'Give yourself credit. All this was possible only because of you. If you hadn't convinced them, we wouldn't be sitting here today.'

They smiled at each other. Then Ajay turned on his heel and walked out. By the time he'd hailed a taxi and was halfway across the city, Sharmaji, Iqbal and Joginder had donned different disguises and were waiting to board their flights.

When Ajay finally reached Mahim, there it was, staring at him from amidst all the garish decor: Priya Weds Badrinath.

It was time for him to claim his woman.

In the hustle and bustle of wedding preparations, nobody noticed a bearded man in a sherwani leaving the premises with his burkha-clad begum – in a taxi headed for the airport.

Mahim, Friday, 6.30 p.m.

I was fifteen minutes too late; there was pandemonium at the wedding venue. Everyone was looking for the bride, who had last been sighted approaching the toilet and had not been seen since. The window panes in the toilet were missing. Clearly her point of exit.

I stepped into the bathroom and looked out on to the road. I was thinking of the choicest abuses for Ajay – and then I thought of something and the laughter welled up inside me again. Back at the hotel, Sharmaji had said, 'Sorry, but I suddenly thought of something Ajju said. He said the man who could catch him hadn't been born yet.'

But I will catch you, you bastard, one day I will, I swore under my breath.

Epilogue

The shrill ringing of a doorbell.

Waseem Khan opened the door to find a postman at the door. His reading glasses were perched on the ridge of his nose and seemed to be precariously held together, the way he peered at the envelope in his hand and asked, 'Waseem saab?'

Waseem nodded.

The postman smiled. 'Sir, you have a money order.'

Waseem was surprised. His brows creased into a frown. Money order. He was sure there was a mistake. He had never received a money order ever in his life. He was reluctant to sign it and take the note the postman proffered. He asked instead, 'Where is it from?

The postman replied, 'Laksmipur. Bhojpur district... Bihar se hai.' Waseem drew a blank even as he tried to figure out who he knew from Laksmipur in Bihar.

Then the postman continued: 'It's a full hundred rupees, and the sender has also written two lines to you.'

Waseem finally decided to accept the money order. There was a two-line message at the bottom: 'Dear Waseem saab, I wanted to return this money personally but I was not able to do so. It is your hard-earned money, it's of no use to me. Yours, Ajay.'

Waseem's jaw dropped. He signed the acknowledgement and was still mulling over the master thief's audacity when his wife called out to him. She was dripping water on the floor after her bath; as usual, she had not towelled her hair dry. She came and stood next to him, near the bed. The towel hung around her waist, sarong style, and her tall, lithe body exuded a floral aroma. Waseem tugged at the towel, pulling it off her waist. He gently pushed her back onto the bed.

This was unfinished business, something that always made him feel years younger. The earlier interruptions had only fuelled his desire. Today, no one would dare to disturb him.

As if on cue, the phone buzzed, just as he bent to down to kiss her.

But this time Waseem was more focused. Nothing in the world could draw him away from the arms of his wife. He picked up the receiver and left it off the hook.

He was totally oblivious to the world. Heaven beckoned.

It was Rahul on the other end, though, and he was loud, and Waseem could still hear him.

Without waiting for a hello from Waseem's end, he said, 'Sir, we've just got a tip-off – they arc in Dubai.'

There went heaven, once again.